Praise for **The Stream**

"When stuck, how do you break free? When blinded from the truth, where is the light? When lost and afraid, what is the test? As you turn each page of this wondrous novel, you travel on your own journey down the stream. Along the twists and turns, you come upon life's eternal questions and find answers to the mystery where you least expect. More than a fantasy or tale, *The Stream* is a way of experiencing the world and learning life lessons. This book is nothing less than a treasure!" Janetti Marotta, PhD, author of *50 Mindful Steps to Self-Esteem: Everyday Practices for Cultivating Self-Acceptance & Self-Compassion*

Praise for A. R. Silverberry's **Wyndano's Cloak**

"**Constant suspense . . . impossible to put down**. You're going to be very tired in the morning!" Feathered Quill Review

"**I loved it!** If you like a tight, well-written, exciting, moving, and, ultimately, satisfying book, then this is for you, regardless of your age and gender." The Book Sage, Review by Lloyd Russell

"**A powerful coming-of-age story** . . . a rich and subtle metaphor for the power of creativity and courage, the function and purpose of artistic inspiration and enrichment, and the role of fantasy and vision in the human psyche." The US Rev

Lloyd,
I'm so happy the stream
brought us together!
Best,
Peter
(A. R. Silverberry)

The Stream

by

A. R. Silverberry

Tree Tunnel Press
Capitola, CA

Print Edition ISBN - 13: 978-0-9841037-2-0

Print Edition ISBN - 10: 0-9841037-2-4

Kindle Edition (ISBN): 13: 978-0-9841037-0-6

ePub Edition (ISBN): 13: 978-0-9841037-1-3

Published by Tree Tunnel Press, P.O. Box 733, Capitola, CA 95010

First Edition. Printed in the United States of America

0987654321

For Sherry,

for swimming the waters with me.

Prologue

I pulled my old bones from the skiff, swearing for the thousandth time that I should've died long ago. Feeling the years most in my fingers, I tugged my mittens snug, secured the vessel with an awkward knot, and made for the campfire. Half a dozen shadows huddled near the flames, which threw flickering gold upon the surrounding rocks and stream.

I squatted by the fire, turning my hands to warm them, and then fished out the last of my flatbread from my rucksack. I broke off a piece and offered it to the man nearest me.

He surveyed me with steely eyes, which peered from the shadow of a low-pulled hat. "I've got mine," he said, holding up duck still dripping on a spit.

Shrugging, I nibbled my bread — grateful that the fire kept the piercing cold of the night at bay — when a small movement near the rocks caught my eye.

The man beside me nodded toward the rocks, a jumble of stones and boulders that had slid down the hillside. "She's been lurking for days, refuses to come out."

"Can you blame her? It's hard to know who's a friend." I smiled pleasantly.

His face was chiseled granite. "Keep an eye out. Someone's pinching supplies."

"I'll do that."

He reached into his longcoat and removed a flask. I noticed as he uncorked the bottle and took a swig that his fingers were smooth, almost delicate. My survival depends on knowing who sits across from me. I sized him up quickly, mindful that calluses are the price of an honest day's work. He held the bottle out to me.

I shook my head. "Swore off years ago." In truth, I'm certain one more drop would send me to my grave. "A bit of that duck would keep me going."

He held the spitted duck up to the firelight, considering. "What'll you give in return?"

Once, I could have crushed a man like this, large as he was, and taken what I wanted, even with that knife he thought was so cleverly hidden in his boot top. But the bulk of my muscles have withered. Now I rely on my wits, and taking is no longer my way.

I held my hands out, palms up, so he could see the frayed yarn and holes in my mittens. "You see I have little."

He took another swig, and some of the granite seemed to melt from his face. He tore off a drumstick and waved the succulent meat in front of me.

The Stream

I snatched it before he could change his mind. Bringing it to my lips, I inhaled the smoky aroma, all the while watching for that shadow among the rocks. "What am I thinking? I forgot to leave an offering."

"It's your belly," he said with a sneer.

I rose and shambled to the rocks. "I'll just leave a bit," I called back to him. I pretended to put a morsel of meat on top of one of the rocks, and then played at gnawing on the leg. A short time later, I snapped my arm as if tossing the bone and risked a peek at my benefactor. Finding him engrossed in his bottle, I laid the uneaten drumstick on the rock, behind which a shape, like a small animal, cowered.

When I returned to the fire, I licked my fingers and thanked him. A minute later, a child's hand — tiny and pale — reached up from the shelter of rocks and grabbed the meat.

"Must be somefin you can give me," the man said. He must have been tilting that bottle before I arrived; his tongue was thickening with firewater. "Whassin in the rucksack?"

I showed him my bedroll, an empty food sack, and a simple drop line to fish with.

He grumbled, turned away, and like the others, bedded down for the night a short distance away. I stirred the fire, sending up a spray of sparks, and waited. When snoring greeted my ears, I took my bedroll back to where I'd left the meat and whispered into the shadows. "I sleep just as well sitting, and the fire will keep me warm."

She didn't reply. I didn't expect her to. If I'd seen one, I'd seen a hundred like her. Glazed-eyed children left parentless *by the flood that tore our world. Many were as mute as trees. Most died from starvation. Those who hadn't, would. Soon.*

I laid my bedroll on the rock, returned to the fire, and leaned against a broad stump. A short time later, her face appeared, a smudge of red in the flickering light. Then she was gone, taking the blanket with her.

I rose before dawn. A bird piped a few plaintive notes in the distance as I laid down a fresh log and fanned up flames. After warming my hands to ease the stiffness and pain, I took my rucksack, stepped around the still, cocooned campers, and headed for my skiff.

The stream shone liked polished lapis lazuli, the trees along the far shore framing the water with inky silhouettes. Leaving the skiff tethered to the stump, I climbed in and let the rope play out so that the boat drifted soundlessly. When the current had taken me midstream, I tied her fast to hold, and then removed my drop line from the rucksack. No one but bitter experience taught me that fish bite when the bugs come out. I pulled forth two trout in short order, using worms I'd stashed in a jar beneath the seat, and returned to the fire, where I broiled them on a stick above the flames.

When they were succulent and smoky, I stored one in my food bag. The other I took to the rocks where my frightened friend was hiding. Gray had begun to penetrate the shadows. Swaddled in my blanket, only a blond rat's nest was visible, and from within the snarl of hair, wide blue eyes stared up at me. I divided the fish, placed half where she could see it, and leaned against the rock to eat the rest.

The Stream

"Get it while it's hot," I whispered.

She was as still as a statue, so I retreated to consider my options. I needed something that would ease her fright. The sandy campsite held nothing of promise, but with luck, the woods beyond the rocks might provide what I needed. As I stepped into the trees, none of the campers stirred, a testament that more than one flask had circulated last night. I foraged at random and found an area where fire had scorched and cleared the older growth and a stand of birch had moved in. Sitting on a fallen birch, I began to peel the bark to fashion a box. Nothing intricate — I'm no longer nimble. Just two long pieces fastened together with two sticks punched through on both ends. I thought I'd make a small comb for her and was just completing the top of the box when I heard stirring in the ferns behind me. I stepped toward the sound and parted the fronds. Nestled in a tumble of grass and decaying leaves was the prize I needed. As gingerly as I could, I slipped it into the box and covered it.

Deep violet tinged the horizon when I returned to the rocks. She was sitting, clutching a stuffed rabbit — worn and gray with grime — her thumb planted in her mouth like a pink flower. She was no older than seven or eight.

She had folded the blanket and placed it where I'd left it for her. "Keep it," I said, tapping the blanket. I pulled the box from my coat and extended it to her. Scratching came from within, weak, almost halfhearted. "Can you take care of this for me?"

Her eyes, big and guileless, grew larger. She hesitated, then reached for the box.

11

"Careful," I said.

Holding it in her palm, she removed the lid. She gave a little gasp, and her mouth opened wide. She looked up at me and nodded.

"Good," I said. "That's just fine. You watch it during the day, and I'll watch it at night. Maybe you can bring it down to me at sundown."

She stared at me. Her eyelids were swollen, the whites red from crying.

I pointed back to camp. "Well, if you can, stop by."

She looked fearfully where the narrow-eyed man slept.

"Don't worry about him. He's as dumb as they come."

I hoped that would make her smile. It didn't. "Has he hurt you?"

She shook her head.

"Good. And he won't. I'll make sure of that."

She looked at my feeble form. If possible, her thumb plunged deeper into her mouth.

I honestly didn't know how I was going to reach her, but in my years I knew that opportunities came. Sure enough, one did, from an unexpected source. The setting sunlight glittered on the stream like rubies. One of the men had trapped a boar and was roasting it over the fire, which crackled and sputtered from the dripping juices. It would be hours before the meat was done.

While the others chattered idly nearby, the man with the flask had his hat pulled down, and I could see his sullen, narrow eyes, staring at me. "You still owe me for that duck," he said.

I was glad I had already divided and shared my second fish with the girl. "You've seen I have nothing."

He pulled on his mustache, a black slash in the shadows. "Then entertain me, old man."

"Yeah," called another. "Give us a story, Grandpa. I bet you got some yarns."

I gazed past the fire at the stream flowing beyond and saw my chance. "Perhaps I have something to tell."

"What's it about?" asked one of the others.

I could have given many answers. A perilous world. The strength of a man. The unbreakable love of the woman beside him.

I cast my voice so that it would reach the rocks. "The courage of a small boy."

I thought maybe I could lure her as I got going, but to my surprise, I saw her clamber out of hiding and walk toward us. My blanket was rolled under one arm. She clutched the rabbit to one cheek, thumb deep in her mouth. I thought she would stop at the perimeter of firelight, but she marched straight on and sat at my feet, gazing up at me.

"Well, looky here," said the narrow-eyed man. "Our thief, boys. Let's search her."

"I've been wondering what happened to my gloves," said another.

"What would a tiny thing like this do with your gloves?" I asked. "And where's she hiding them, in her bunny?"

The man shrank from the laughter of his buddies.

"I still say it's her," said the narrow-eyed man.

I smiled, pleasantly. "I've shown you what's in my rucksack. It's only fair that everyone show us what's in theirs."

"Leave off, Cleef," someone called. "Let's hear the story."

Cleef's eyes shrank to slits.

"You could check where she's been hiding," I said.

He stalked to the rocks. While he was nosing around, the girl lifted her blanket enough for me to see the box I'd given her. Faint scratching came from within.

Cleef returned with a scowl. "Get on with your story, old man."

The girl gazed up at me. This was no bedtime story, but I hoped it would be medicine. For her and for me.

I began, "Wend's world was a watery snake."

Chapter One

The Storm

From atop the bosun's chair, Wend watched as the current twisted and rolled, setting the sloop to pitch and tug at the mooring lines. He glanced at the horizon. Dark clouds reared above the trees like an angry god.

His father circled the deck below, securing lines. "Stow your toys," he called to Wend.

Wend was already moving, scrambling down the mast and snatching up toys every five-year-old had: a boat; a fishing rod; a few fish; a mother, father, and children, carved from wood. He carried them down the steps and into the cabin, where he tossed them into a basket, closed the lid, and tied it securely. Returning topside, he looked around the boat. His mother was grabbing fish from the drying rack and throwing them into a burlap sack. His father grasped the anchor rope. He wore a vest, open at the chest, with no shirt beneath, and his arm muscles bulged as he brought up the anchor.

"Wend, lend a hand here," said his father.

Wend scurried over and pitched in. He doubted he was adding much, but it made him feel big to be heaving beside his father.

"Where are we taking her?" asked his father when they'd weighed anchor.

The sloop was in the middle of the river, which was about a quarter mile wide. Wend scanned the nearer shore for safe harbor and spied a willow with a majestic trunk leaning toward the water. He pointed to the tree. "Tie her there, nose in."

"Good man." His father ruffled Wend's hair, which fell in wandering streams to his neck.

Fat drops began smacking the deck. A crosscurrent jarred the boat, turning it forty degrees, and Wend stumbled. "Is it a bad one?" he asked.

His father grinned. "What does a man do?"

The question was part of a game they played. "Ride it for all it's worth," Wend replied.

His father waved an arm toward the stream. "It's all a wild ride, Wend. Let's pull the beard of this storm and laugh in its face!" As if to show he meant it, his booming laughter drowned out the wind, now whistling and howling about the boat.

"I'll get the paddles," said Wend.

"No, help your mother."

"But you said—"

"Do you see those rollers?" His father pointed at the waves barreling down on them. "One of those might sweep you overboard. What does a man do?"

"Protect his family."

"What kind of man would I be if I let you go overboard?"

"But I want to be with you."

"Jibe-ho, Wend."

"Yes, sir."

For sailors, jibe-ho meant it was time to change direction away from resistance. Wend turned to look for his mother. She wasn't topside. He leaned against the wind as he stepped to the cabin. At the entrance, he turned to look at the stream. Rain pocked the surface. The water seemed to have risen, threatening to invade the forest that marched down on both shores. Above, roiling clouds blocked the sun. Thunder rumbled in the distance. The worst was coming.

He found his mother in the cabin, loading a wicker basket with pots, pans, plates, and utensils.

"Finish picking up here," she said.

"But I want to help you and Dad."

"Do as you're told." Debate was over when she used that voice.

"Is it a bad one?"

His mother stared at him. Her hair was pulled back into a knot. Wind penetrating the cabin blew strands that had come loose. "We'll get through it."

Her eyes told him the truth. She squatted before him, her gaze wandering over him from head to foot. "Let me look at you. I want to make sure no one switched my son."

This was the game his mother played, even now, with the wind roaring, and the boat pitching and yawing, and fear he had never seen before in those gray eyes.

"Let's see," she said. "Hair the color of wet earth." She ran her fingers through his hair and it flopped back in disarray. She picked up one of his arms. "Sun-brown skin. Streaks of dirt running up and down your legs. But what about those eyes?" She leaned forward, scrutinizing. "Flecks of sky, earth, and trees. That would be my Wend." She hugged him tighter than she ever had before. Rising, she wagged a finger at him. "I want this cabin shipshape."

"Yes, ma'am."

Wend watched her go up the stairs and close the door behind her. He scanned the cabin. His mother had been cutting mushrooms for soup. He dumped the mushrooms into a sack and fastened it with string. Then he put the sack into a bin beneath the table. He tipped water from a jug almost his size onto a dishcloth and wiped the knife. When it was clean, he dried it and put it away. Then he cleaned, dried, and put away the chopping board. He pushed the water jug beneath the table and tied it to a table leg. The table and three chairs were nailed to the floor. They weren't going anywhere.

He peeked out of one of the windows. It had been bright not long ago. Now it was almost as dark as night. Rain pelted the stream. Two dozen yards away, another sloop tottered like a drunken sailor, and a wave rolled over its bow. Wend closed the window and latched it.

His father was yelling. Wend couldn't make out the words, but he could guess what was going on. His father was paddling to that willow. If he could tie the boat down at the shore, they'd be safer.

Storm, flood, rapids, waterfall. Every man, woman, and child in the stream knew these words. Wend said them almost as soon as he'd learn to say mama and papa. He'd seen floods, storms, and rapids. He'd only heard about waterfalls.

His father said a waterfall was when the world tipped ninety degrees, and the stream fell out from under you. For years, the idea gave Wend nightmares.

The wind howled around their little boat. From the sound, Wend judged the strength of the storm, confirming his mother's look.

It was dark as night now. Lightning flashed. Wend counted to five and heard a deep, ominous rumble. The boat was tipping back and forth, and Wend had to hang on to the table to keep from rolling across the floor.

His father should have gotten to shore by now, into shallow water, away from the current. Wend wanted to be with him. He knew he couldn't help, but he longed to be held, to have his trembling soothed. He emptied clothes out of a big basket and tucked them under his bedding. Then he tied the basket to hooks along the cabin wall, climbed in, and closed the lid over him.

A master basket maker, his mother had woven this one from cordage grass. "Strong and watertight," she would tell him. "That's what you want on the stream."

A flash of lightning shone through the translucent fiber. He hugged himself and thought of the last time his mother had held him. Before the sun had risen, he'd climbed into their bed and into his mother's arms. His head was tucked beneath her chin, and she'd kissed him. Soon after, his father had taken him topside. He'd sat on his father's lap while his father tossed out the fishing line.

"Teach me to fish," Wend had said.

"When you're a little older, and stronger than the fish."

Then his father had sung a song to make Wend strong. Wend hummed it now, hummed it while the wind wailed and the basket tipped at frightening angles. For a moment, he thought he heard his father singing the song too, a bitter taunt in the wind. Wend sang out loud, to make his father strong.

The Stream

Thunder exploded over the boat. The basket swayed, throwing Wend against its side, the grooves pressing into his cheek.

Another explosion and a terrifying ripping, and Wend knew the boat was breaking apart.

Chapter Two

The Trick

Wend couldn't say how long the basket had rolled and twirled in the current, how long waves had crashed over him, or how long the wind shrieked. He hugged his knees and thought about his parents and their boat. The boat was gone, or he wouldn't be bobbing in the stream like a cork. But maybe his parents had survived. His father was strong and smart, and so was his mother. They could have swum for shore. They could be searching for him now. First chance he got, he would go back and look for them.

The hope of finding his parents calmed the terror churning inside, and he fell asleep.

He dreamed he was sitting on his father's lap. His father was fishing and sang the song to make Wend stronger. His father's rumbling baritone changed to a hoarse tenor. The dream dissolved. As he awoke, Wend realized someone else was singing, the voice rising above the dull roar of the stream.

The basket was still. He rubbed his legs to get the circulation flowing. Then he pushed open the lid and stood.

The basket had come to rest on a sandy, treelined shore. The stream, swollen with muddy water and branches, flowed swiftly. An old man sat on a raft, making no attempt to steer. As he drew near, he looked at Wend and stopped singing. "You survived the storm," he called.

Wend nodded. "Have you seen my mom and dad?"

"I've seen no one but you, and many broken boats."

"Our boat is gone."

"So I see, but that basket is handy. You must be hungry."

Wend nodded. The old man stood and began poling toward Wend. He wore a loose-fitting shirt, and his pants fell to knobby knees. Wend was surprised that someone so thin could pole with such strength, but as the old man approached, Wend saw wiry muscles in his arms and legs.

When he reached the shore, the old man hopped off and dragged the raft halfway from the water. Aside from the pole, he had an angler's creel, fishing pole, and knife. Nothing more. He carried the creel and knife to a level spot on the shore and set them down. Then he walked over to Wend and lifted him out of the basket.

"Help me find wood," said the old man.

They collected wood. Most was still wet from the storm, but they found some dry pieces under a pile of branches and bark that the wind had blown beneath a leafless catalpa tree.

"Do you know how to build a fire?" the old man asked, dropping an armload of wood beside his basket.

Wend nodded and began breaking sticks. When the fire was crackling, the old man took a water jug and a small pot from his basket. He poured water into the pot and set it on the fire. Then he took a large fish from the basket and began cleaning it with his knife.

"The stream brings gifts today." He smiled. His teeth were white, but the left front one was chipped. "Go see what you can find while I cook this."

Wend went to the shore. Refuse from broken boats floated by. Most of it was worthless. He saw a good, sound oar, but it was too far away. After awhile, a water jug came bobbing toward him. When it was close enough to reach, he snagged it. He removed the cork and found fresh water inside. He set the jug aside and continued watching the stream. Nothing more of value drifted by, so he brought the jug back to the fire and sat.

The old man looked at the jug. "Good. That is useful." He took the pot off the fire with his shirtsleeve. "Too bad you didn't find a bowl. I only have one." He took a wooden bowl from his basket and poured in half of the broth. Then he cut the fish, put half in the bowl, and handed it to Wend. "I'll eat mine from the pot."

"Do you have any spoons?"

"I lost my other basket in the storm." The old man grinned. "Maybe the stream will bring us spoons."

They sipped their broth, and when it was cool enough, ate the fish with their fingers.

"What do you want today?" the old man asked.

The question surprised Wend, but he knew the answer. He pointed upstream. "I'm going back to find my parents."

The old man pondered him. The wrinkles in his face were deep and looked like ripples. "You can't."

"Why not?"

"Because we're here."

"Why can't I be there?"

"Because you can't."

"Can you take me?"

"No, I'm here too."

Wend set down his empty bowl. "What if they're alive and looking for me?"

"I hope so, but you can't go upstream."

Wend recalled a time when his family's boat got stuck in mud. His father had kicked the side of the boat and cried, "Move, you stubborn pile of timber." The boat didn't move until it rained and the stream picked up the boat and cast it off again. Now Wend felt just as stubborn as that boat. He rose. "I'm going back."

"Well, take your water jug."

Wend washed the bowl in the stream and returned it to the old man.

"You can have it if you want," said the old man.

"Then you won't have one."

"The stream brought that one. It will bring another."

Wend shook his head. "You already gave me fish. I'll give you my basket for your bowl and basket."

"That is good. Your basket will weigh you down."

The old man's basket was small enough for Wend to carry. He put in his water jug and bowl and secured the lid. After saying farewell to the old man, he followed the shore upstream. The shoreline zigzagged, and soon the old man was out of sight.

The day was bright and warm. Birds sang among the alders and maples to his left. No cloud marred the sky. Hope swelled in his breast that he would find his parents. He rounded a bend in the shore and saw an old man sitting with his back against a leafless tree. Wend stopped in his tracks. He could swear it was the same old man he'd just left. He glanced behind, bewildered, and then he approached the old man. The old man's eyes were half-lidded, and he gazed at the stream. Wend waited to be acknowledged, but the old man was motionless. His raft was still halfway up the bank. The big basket Wend had traded, the cooking pot, and the knife were beside the fire, which had burned low.

The Stream

It's a trick, Wend thought, and he stomped off, following the sandy shore upstream. The shore zigzagged, he rounded a turn, and again saw the old man sitting beneath the tree. This time the fire had burned to embers.

I'm dreaming, Wend thought. *I'm in my bed in the boat, and I'll wake up and see my mom and dad.*

Dream or not, he had to keep trying. Walking on the shore hadn't worked, so he waded into the water and plowed upstream. He occupied his thoughts thinking about his mother and father. His father would be cutting timber to make a new boat. His mother would be gathering mushrooms by the shore, and a big pot of stew would be waiting for Wend, just around that turn.

But around that turn, Wend found the same spot he'd left behind him. The fire was out.

The old man was gone.

Chapter Three

Leena

Night shrouded the clearing. Strange crashing sounds came from the forest. Wend shivered and wished he still had the big basket. He could have slept in that, and kept warm and out of sight. He imagined monsters stalking through the trees, the way he'd imagined monsters rising from the stream and reaching into the boat with long tentacles — tentacles to snatch him from bed and drag him underwater. If he woke up and shadows played about the cabin, he'd crawl into bed with his parents.

His mother always knew how to comfort him. He ached for her now.

A terrifying thought sprouted in his mind. What if his parents perished in the storm? He tried to push it away, but it grew larger than the monsters in the forest.

What if he was alone?

The Stream

The question nipped and snapped at him for hours, until at last he fell asleep. When he awoke, the sun was rising. Daylight brought hope, and a new idea. He could go upstream through the forest. The shore and the stream had tricked him, but maybe he could reach his parents by going through the trees.

The forest seemed normal now. The monsters would be asleep.

He went down to the stream, washed, and turned to face the forest. All was quiet, save for the sound of a squirrel packing nuts into a knothole. Wend took a deep breath, held it a moment, and marched into the trees.

He could think of only one place to look for his parents. Near that majestic willow. He wondered how far he had drifted during the storm, and how long it would take to find that tree.

It didn't matter. The path led to a clearing. The same clearing where he'd spent the night.

I can't go back . . . he realized with terrifying clarity. *I can't ever go back.*

He sank beside the dead fire and cried. When no more tears would fall, he pondered what to do. *If I can't go to them, maybe they'll find me. I'd better stay put.*

He sat, hummed the strengthening song, and waited. Stream people drifted by on their boats. One, a sky-blue houseboat with pink trim around the windows, was a beauty. On a deck built above the cabin, a man was cutting away a piece of tattered awning. On a lower deck beyond the cabin, a woman and a little girl were making baskets in the shade of a broad umbrella. Looking up from her work, the girl tugged on her mother's sleeve and pointed at Wend.

"Are you lost?" the woman called.

"I'm waiting for my parents," Wend yelled back. "They're in the forest making a new boat."

The woman looked doubtfully at the trees, but continued weaving. The girl stepped to the bow, where she sat and stared at Wend. Her hair was long, flowing, and blue-black, like the stream at night. Wend watched her until the boat drifted from sight.

Five monks rounded the bend on a boat fashioned from reeds. Wend had seen monks before. They wore bright orange robes, and sang to drums and rattles made from gourds.

A monk called to Wend, "Are you okay?"

"My father is building a new boat in the forest."

The man smiled blissfully. "A boat will take you to the Great Ocean."

Wend watched them drift on, but his thoughts were on a conversation he'd had with his father.

"Where does the stream come from?" Wend had asked.

"The source."

"Where's that?"

His father pointed upstream.

"Where does the stream go?"

"Some say it pours into a great ocean, and we'll feel peace and joy when we get there."

"What do you think?"

"I think you'd better finish coiling that rope."

Other boats drifted by. People were broiling fish, pounding acorns for flour, and drying persimmons.

The water in the stream still looked muddy from the storm. Wend sipped sparingly from his water jug. He would have to find fresh water soon. And food. He hadn't eaten since yesterday, and the hole in his stomach was growing.

At last, hunger lashed him into the forest to search for food. He couldn't find fruit or nuts, but he found mushrooms growing about the base of a cottonwood. He'd watched his mother gather them. She'd told him about good mushrooms and the ones that make you sick. These were white, like the ones his mother gathered, so he picked them and returned to his spot beside the stream.

He ate the mushrooms and watched the boats go by, hoping his parents would be on one of them. A kick in the stomach announced he'd picked the wrong mushrooms. Wend vomited and spent the rest of the afternoon running for the bushes. His trips gave him no relief. It felt like a snake was eating its way out of his stomach. He was exhausted when the pain let up and fell into a deep sleep.

❖

Wend had the sensation that he was being carried.

Mother, he thought. *She's found me.*

Sleep melted away. An orange-robed monk carried Wend up a ramp and onto a boat.

"I'm waiting for my parents." Wend's arm felt as heavy as a boulder, but he pointed to the trees. "They're in the forest."

"We're looking now," replied the monk. His head was shaved, and he was so thin he seemed to disappear inside the folds of his robe. "Are you hungry?" he asked.

Wend nodded. The monk went into the cabin, made of woven rattan walls and a thatched roof. Wavy blue lines had been painted the length of the deck, where rattles, drums, and four mats were arranged in a semicircle. Wend caught these details in a glance. His attention was riveted on the trees. Three monks stepped from the foliage and crossed the beach toward the boat. The first was short and plump, and his orange robe swelled about the middle. The second monk's head was shaved like the others but was so smooth it shone. The third was old, but his face was bright and round as the moon.

Wend's mind raced. What would he say when they reported finding no sign of his parents?

They walked up the ramp and sat before Wend on the mats. The thin monk emerged from the cabin with a tray of food. He handed Wend an empty bowl and a cup of water. "Drink slowly," he said.

He served his companions. They rose with their bowls, and then they all stood single file before Wend.

The thin monk was first. His bowl contained a single spoonful of fish, which he slipped into Wend's bowl.

"You gave me yours," said Wend.

The monk ruffled Wend's hair and smiled. "*She* gives me all I need. Call me Skinny."

Wend giggled. "Is that really your name?"

Skinny touched the tip of Wend's nose. "And why not, if it brings a smile to a boy's face?"

Second in line was the plump monk. "Call me Wonder." He also gave Wend his spoonful of fish, then placed a finger to his lips. A piece of dried apple dropped from his sleeve and into Wend's bowl.

Next, the shiny-headed monk gave his morsel of fish.

"Why is your head so shiny?" Wend asked him.

"I shave it twice a day."

"Why?"

"It brings me closer to *Her*. Call me Shine."

Wend grinned from ear to ear.

Last, the old monk shook his bit of fish into Wend's bowl. "My name is long forgotten." He chuckled. Returning to his mat, he watched Wend eat.

"You all gave me yours," said Wend.

The four monks slapped each other on the back and laughed.

Wend finished the meal far too soon. After Shine cleared away the bowls, he walked to the side of the boat and began drawing up the ramp. Wend leaped to his feet. A wave of dizziness made him stagger. Despite his size, Wonder was beside him in a moment, and kept him from falling.

"I've got to get ashore," Wend cried.

"We looked," said Wonder. "You're alone."

"But I'm waiting for my parents." He watched with desperation as Shine shoved the boat into the stream with a pole.

The old monk knelt beside Wend. His voice was gentle, like falling rain. "Did you lose them in the storm?"

Wend slumped against the cabin and nodded. "You have a boat. You can take me upstream to look for them."

"That would take us from our path," said the old monk. "We are going to the Great Ocean."

"But that will take me away from them."

He held Wend's hand. "We see everyone who is on the stream. If they are alive, we will meet them."

The boat was skimming along the middle of the stream now, and Wend felt too faint to argue. The monks brought him acacia boughs to rest upon, and soon he fell asleep in the warm sun.

The Stream

❖

The sun was setting when he awoke. The boat was anchored at the shore. Other boats had stopped there too, and the owners had built a fire. The aroma of roast duck filled the air.

"We stop for food," said the old monk. "You're still weak. We'll bring you some."

The four monks took their bowls, slipped over the side of the boat, and walked toward the families gathered by the fire. They stopped a short distance away and bowed their heads. The people by the fire approached the monks and put food into their bowls. When the monks returned to the boat, they shared with Wend what they had received.

Wend loved duck, and after savoring his portion of meat, he sucked and chewed on a piece of crispy fat. "Why do you beg?" he asked the old monk.

The monk waved a hand toward the crowd on the shore. "The Great Ocean blesses these people for feeding Her children."

"Don't you fish?"

"Our hearts and minds are focused on the Great Ocean. By devoting ourselves wholly to that, we reach Her sooner."

Wend frowned. "But you're here. How can you be someplace you haven't got to?"

"Our bodies are here, but our minds are on the Great Ocean."

"Have you seen it?"

"When I'm meditating deeply, I see it clearly."

"What does it look like?"

The monk's eyes grew bright. "Rainbows shimmer in Her waters. No waves ruffle Her surface, which are as smooth as glass, and people dance on clouds of joy."

Next morning, Wend scrutinized each boat they passed in hope of finding his parents, while Skinny, Shine, and Wonder knelt on mats and closed their eyes. The old monk sat at the tiller, studying Wend. At last he said, "Only a drop of us is on the stream. The rest lies in the Great Ocean. That's why we're in bliss when we return there."

Wend pointed at the kneeling monks. "Are they sleeping?"

"They are meditating. Focus all your attention on the Ocean and the stream disappears. There is only the Ocean."

"I need to watch for my parents."

"You haven't lost them, Wend. They are in the Great Ocean, waiting for you."

That night, the monks took out drums and rattles. They sang and danced around the boat with such abandon that Wend feared they would crash into each other. The beat on their drums and rattles quickened, and soon they were whirling and spinning. Their robes billowed, and it seemed they would float off.

The Stream

The old monk set down his drum and grasped both of Wend hands. Next thing he knew, Wend was flying around the boat with them. He threw back his head until the stars were dizzy streaks.

The old monk cried, "Can you see the Ocean, Wend? Can you see it? Your parents are there."

Days passed peacefully. Wend was given robes and instructed on how to kneel and focus on the Great Ocean. The old monk assured Wend he would see his parents there. Wend wasn't sure he saw the Ocean, but he could picture his parents' faces and recalled swimming with them. One summer they'd caught a goose that his mother had roasted slowly on a spit. When the old monk asked Wend if he'd seen his parents, he could truthfully say he had. The memories gave him comfort. He didn't care that his knees were sore, and the old monk was pleased with his progress.

Wend was given a begging bowl and taught how to stand with head bowed while people dropped fruit, nuts, and bits of fish into his bowl. "Never look at them," Wonder told him. "Remain humble."

One day, they stopped by a large gathering of boats moored beside a sandy spit. Several fires had been started, and on one of them a goat was roasting over the flames. When the meat was well browned and dripping amber, the monks lined up and stood with bowed heads. Monks from other boats joined them, and Wend was at the end of the line.

Each time someone dropped a morsel into his bowl, Wend said, "The Ocean's blessings upon you."

After the fifth or sixth blessing, Wend became aware that someone stood before him but had not offered food. It was all he could do to keep his feet still and his head down.

At last, he could stand it no more and risked a peek. It was the girl with the blue-black hair. A half smile curled her lips. Her eyes were as bright as gems, and unwavering. Wend decided she was the most beautiful thing he'd ever seen, but he remembered his lessons and quickly looked down.

"You're the boy on the bank," she said.

Wend remained silent, trying to appear as humble as he could.

"Now you're the boy in orange robes."

Wend waited.

"Your parents are dead."

"They aren't," he whispered, hoping the monks wouldn't hear him, but sparks of anger shot inside him.

"They are, or you wouldn't be in robes. My parents say all monks are orphans, and their parents were killed in storms, rapids, and waterfalls."

"That's a lie." Wend flung his bowl aside and leaped on the girl. They fell to the ground, where they rolled and pummeled each other in a cloud of dust.

"My parents don't lie," she yelled. She was an inch taller and wrestled him onto his back.

"Take it back," Wend cried, "take it back."

The monks pulled her off him. As they whisked him back to the boat, he could hear her screaming, "I won't take it back. I won't."

His face grave, the old monk sat beside Wend on the deck. The monks had been kind and never laid a hand on him. He expected a thrashing now.

"Wend, when one of us gets angry, it slows the journey of all to the Ocean. Do you understand?"

Wend nodded.

"When you're wrapped in ropes of the past, you can't see the future. Meditate on that until the stream disappears."

Wend tried to meditate, but he couldn't get the girl out of his mind. It wasn't just what she'd said. He felt an odd flutter in the pit of his stomach.

Late that afternoon, the monks made Wend beg until his bowl was full, and then he was sent to the girl's boat to apologize. He would have preferred the thrashing. His left eye had swelled, and he didn't want to show the girl proof that she'd beaten him.

The houseboat was moored on a placid strip of water between the spit and the shore. The girl's father was brushing sky-blue paint onto the bow, the muscles in his bare back rippling with each stroke.

Wend stood at the bottom of the ramp and called, "The blessings of the Ocean on you and your family."

The man wiped his brow, streaking paint onto an old woolen cap. "Courtin', are you? A coat of paint and a few nails, son. That's how you win 'em."

The burn spread from Wend's ears to the bottom of his neck. "I'm . . . here to apologize. Is your daughter home?"

"Climb aboard, son."

Wend crossed the ramp and onto the lower deck, where the girl's mother was grinding pepper beneath a yellow umbrella. She had copper hair, worn loose, and eyebrows plucked into neat arches.

Wend handed the bowl of food to her. "The blessings of the Ocean on you and your family. I'm sorry I hit your daughter."

"I don't know what to do with that girl." The woman snatched a kerchief from her bodice and dabbed her eyes. "I've told her and told her. Fighting like a tomcat. How will she ever catch a strong man? Stubborn, stubborn girl. She never listens to her dear mother."

"I started it."

"Never you mind. She'll spend two days in the cabin. And *she* can apologize." She cupped her hands and called, "Leena!"

Footsteps rushed in the cabin. The door was flung wide. Leena burst through the opening, crying, "I knew you couldn't shut me —" She skidded to a halt, her eyes shooting bolts at Wend.

"Apologize to him," said her mother.

Leena folded her arms. "I won't."

Her mother grabbed Leena's arm, dragged her until she faced Wend, and gave her a shake. "Apologize."

"Never." Leena yanked her arm away, sending her hair flying in wild tangles.

"Apologize, or you'll spend the next week scrubbing deck."

"I'll scrub."

Her mother fetched a pail, filled it with stream water, and set it down beside a brush. "Get started."

Leena reached for the brush, victory bright on her face.

"No. Wait," cried Wend. "I started it. I hurt the monks, and now I'm getting you in trouble. I came to say I'm sorry." He'd forgotten what had angered him. She was a strange, mysterious creature that held him entranced. He wanted to be close to her, watch how her hair billowed with a mind of its own, and study the faint mud stains that ran up her arms and legs like rivers and streams.

He held out his hand. "I'm Wend."

She stared at him for the longest time with eyes like stars. At last she took his hand. Her touch was light, but it sent a charge through him.

"Sorry," she said, kissed his cheek, and darted back to the cabin.

Over the next days, Wend thought of nothing but the kiss. He touched where her lips brushed his cheek. He saw her blazing eyes and hair like night. She was on his mind when he went to sleep, when he awoke, when he was supposed to be focusing on the Ocean. The cloud of worry about his parents receded. The monks must have seen it. They were pleased and told him he was progressing rapidly. He danced with them at night, but instead of seeing the Ocean, blue-black hair flew like wings about him, and her eyes were the brightest stars.

He looked for his parents in the boats that passed, but he also looked for Leena. He thought he saw her once or twice, but other houseboats floated downstream, and it was too far away to tell. One afternoon, the monks moored their boat near an island by the head of a tributary. Knots of people crowded around half a dozen fire pits, and Wend could smell fish, wrapped in fig leaves, smoking beneath the flames. He'd barely set foot ashore when he saw her weaving through a crowd, chasing a puppy. It was all Wend could do to keep from dashing after them.

The old monk tapped him on the shoulder. "Heart and mind on the Ocean, Wend, heart and mind."

Wend stood in line with his bowl, beside the old monk. He hadn't eaten since yesterday, but the hole in his stomach vanished. His attention was focused, and it wasn't on the Ocean. The dog was chasing Leena, and as she flitted about the beach, she saw Wend. The dog leaped and barked around her, but she'd stopped, and no longer seemed to see it. She ran to her boat. A short time later she approached the monks. Wend watched surreptitiously as she walked down the line and dropped food into each monk's bowl. When she got to the old monk, she said, "Can Wend play?"

Wend held his breath, focusing his attention on a fly walking the edge of his bowl.

When the monk didn't answer, Leena asked, "Didn't you ever want to play when you were little?"

The old monk sighed. "Bring him back by nightfall."

Leena grabbed Wend's hand. He went flying after her.

"First, we eat," said Leena. She led Wend by the hand along a trail through a meadow. Her other hand held a picnic basket her mother had fixed for them.

"How about there?" Wend asked, pointing to a pear tree.

She ran in reply, pulling him along through a field of bluets and spring beauties. When they reached the tree, they sat and arranged the food before them. Smoked duck, walnut orange relish, wild rice, apple cider, and date candies crusted in bee pollen, which

A. R. Silverberry

they'd prepared on Leena's boat. To Wend, it was a banquet—greater than any he'd had with his parents. When he thought about them, he felt as if the ground had fallen away beneath his feet and he was tumbling into deep, empty darkness. But during the past hour, the hole had filled in, its sides softened, and light streamed in. Leena's father, Skip, had shown Wend how to clean catfish. And Ketty, her mother, talked with him as if she'd known him for years. They made him feel that their boat was his boat.

Leena poured cider into two earthenware cups. "What's it like being a monk?"

"We sing and dance a lot."

"What will you do when you grow up?"

"Fish."

"You can't fish if you're a monk."

Wend hadn't thought of that.

Leena cut breast meat off the duck and handed it to Wend. "Have you fished?" she asked.

"A little," he lied.

Leena looked him up and down. "You couldn't pull a minnow."

Wend blushed. He'd only eaten one meal a day with the monks. He was down to skin and bones.

"Don't worry," she said. "I'm going to fatten you up."

She nibbled around the wishbone, and then held it up, clean. "We'll make a wish, later."

The Stream

With a pang, Wend thought of his parents and his three attempts to return to that majestic willow. "Did you know, we can only go that way?" He pointed downstream.

"Everyone knows that, silly. Except a few miles upstream or away from the shores. My father says we're tied to the stream like fish."

Wend took a long draft of cider to cover embarrassment that he had not understood this sooner. Leena didn't seem to notice. She poured him another glass of cider and spooned onto his plate a helping of walnut orange relish.

When they were done eating, they pretended they were on their own boat. Wend fished with a stick he snapped off the tree. Leena took reeds from the basket and began weaving. Her fingers were nimble and quick. Soon, she'd made a bracelet.

"You'll make strong baskets," he said.

She handed the bracelet to him. "It's unbreakable."

Wend tested the bracelet, pulling it in different directions. The weave was tight. She helped him put it on his wrist. Her finger lingered against his thumb and felt warm. His thumb tingled.

She jumped up. "Come on, I'll race you to the stream. We'll swim to the island."

In a flash, she was twenty feet ahead. He caught up with her at the shore and gazed at the island. The current rushed swiftly, twirling a log as if it were a toy.

"Maybe we shouldn't," he said.

"We should. We're going to fight pirates," she cried and plunged into the water.

She swam with powerful strokes and waved when she reached the island. The sting of losing his fight with her urged him into the water; he wasn't going to be outdone.

They explored the island and found a rock for their boat. They stored pebbles for food. A tree limb was their tiller. Wind rippling the grass was the current. And stones were fish that Wend pulled up with his fishing pole.

"These waters are home to pirates and thieves," said Leena. "They'll slit your throat for a pot of stew, and throw you overboard just to watch you drown. I'll take first watch." A moment later, she cried, "Avast! Here come the river rats now! Grab your knife, or we're fish bait."

Wend grabbed his stick, and he and Leena battled pirates to the death.

The sun dipped toward the horizon, ending the day too soon. They returned to the picnic spot and packed their basket. Leena cleaned the wishbone with her shirt, placed her thumb on one side, and held out the other for Wend.

"Make a wish," she said, "but don't say what it is, or it won't come true."

"Can I make two?"

"Sure, but make them good ones."

Wend held his side of the bone tightly and closed his eyes. He saw his parents, as clearly as if they were before him. And another day with Leena.

"One, two, three, *pull*," said Leena.

Wend pulled. The bone snapped and he opened his eyes. He held the length of the bone from his side. Leena held the length from her side. The centerpiece had fallen between their feet.

Leena picked up the bone and dropped it into Wend's palm. "Keep it," she said, "To remember me."

Chapter Four

Rapids

Aboard their boat one day, the monks taught Wend the Stone Dance. They pinned their robes above their knees, held out their hands, and tipped from side to side, as if trying to keep balance.

The steps were hard to follow at first, but the old monk explained them. "Pretend you are in the stream, Wend. The water is gentle, caressing your ankles as it flows. The bottom of the stream is covered with slippery stones. You rock to the left so you don't fall." The old man spread his arms like wings and tipped. "You rock to the right. Watch out! There's a river snake swimming between the rocks. Lift your knee or he'll bite."

Wend followed along, imagining a snake winding between the rocks. He lifted his knee until the snake passed.

The Stream

The monk threw up his hands in ecstasy. "Look! Half buried in the mud. A blaze of light." He bent, pretending to scoop something up, and raised his hand aloft. "Do you know what this is, Wend?"

"A rock?"

"Yes, at first it will appear that way, but the stream rolls and breaks and polishes it until all that's left is a perfect cut diamond. Look inside, Wend. Do you see? It's a piece of the ocean."

Wend liked the dance. When he held the stone aloft, he didn't see the ocean glimmering within; he saw the magical day he'd spent with Leena. He looked for her many days among the boats drifting downstream, but she wasn't among them. Wend guessed that her parents had lingered by the island, where fish were plentiful.

The monks never lingered. The ocean could be around the next bend, waiting with open arms.

Once, Wend saw a man with a shaggy beard chopping wood near the riverbank. The man didn't have a boat, but a log cabin was nestled in the trees nearby, and smoke rose from the chimney.

"Why doesn't he have a boat?" Wend asked the old monk.

"He doesn't see the stream."

"Why not?"

"He's forgotten that it's there. Such a man is far from the Ocean."

❖

Flowers wilted and dried on the hillsides. The sun seemed to hang motionless in the sky, blasting fire. The stream shrank, and sometimes the boat grazed rocks on the bottom. The monks retreated into the cabin and fanned themselves with ferns to escape the heat and mosquitoes.

"Our journey slows, Wend. This is a sad time for us," said the old monk.

The stream slowed, but it moved. Even when their boat was stuck, streamlets wound among the rocks. Leaves — gold, carmine, and umber — fell into the water and floated downstream.

Fish left with the leaves. The monks lived on nuts, dried fruit, and roots. Only when the trees were skeletons did the rains come. Crashing music flooded the streambed and lifted the boat. Seizing their drums and rattles, the monks sang, leaped, and twirled about the deck. The old monk snatched Wend and lifted him onto his shoulders. Wend laughed, and reaching for the sky, caught the falling drops in his mouth.

Wend was asleep when the boat hit the rapids. He was thrown out of bed and rolled across the cabin. Staggering to his feet, he gripped the banister and pulled himself upstairs to the deck.

"Stay below," Wonder yelled.

"I can help," Wend cried.

The Stream

The water was no longer their friend. It was a monster, laughing, daring them to slide down its back. The boat was tossed and thrown. Water erupted over the deck. Geysers drenched them. The deck was as slippery as ice, but Wend grabbed the drums and rattles and stored them below. He fastened down baskets. Then there was nothing more to do but hold on and hope.

Rocks jutted up, sharp, immovable. The water turned into foamy chaos and sheets of white and spray. It plunged into the boat left and right, and bounced and turned it in circles. The stream hissed and boiled like a witch's cauldron.

Waves beat the boat underwater. Wend held his breath until it surfaced. A mountain of water reared up and plunged them under again. When they resurfaced, Wonder was no longer at the rudder. Wend spotted him bobbing in the water. Wonder reached out one arm to them. Then he was rolling in the waves. Then he was gone.

A colossal wave picked up the boat and flung it. It sailed through the air and crashed onto a rock thrusting from the water like a giant tooth. The boat broke like tinder. Wend tumbled into the stream. He fought for air as he was twirled and carried down a series of cascades. He latched on to a piece of the boat. He saw a flash of orange, and wondered which monk it was, and if he was alive.

Wend hugged the board tight. The stream could do what it liked. He was not going to let go. The current swirled and twisted, carrying him as much backward as forward. It could throw him if it wanted to, but he wasn't going to let go.

And then the board struck a rock and Wend did let go, shaken loose like a leaf. He was whisked downstream through a gorge. The current was swift, but the water went from white to blue. Wend was carried to the side of the gorge. He grabbed on to a root extending from the rock wall.

A hundred feet away, the old monk bobbed in the water. He reached out an arm.

"Let go," he called to Wend. "She's taking us home."

Wend held tight to the water-blackened root and watched as the monk was submerged in another churning rapid.

The root sprang from the rock a foot above the water. Wend worked his way, arm over arm, until he got to the rock. The side was steep, almost vertical, and covered with wet moss. Wend looked for fingerholds and tried to climb out. The fingerholds were too small, the rock too slick, and he slipped back down.

The stream was bone-numbing cold. He needed to get out of the water, and fast. He lurched up and grabbed on to a hanging fern. The fern snapped in his hand. Over the next few minutes, he sent half a dozen fronds downstream. He watched the current carry them away, convinced at last he was not going up the rock.

He wondered if the monks were dead. Before, the thought that his parents were still alive comforted him. He had looked for them among the passing boats as much as he'd looked for Leena. But hope that they were alive faded as the leaves fell into the water and passed downstream.

The thought that the monks were dead filled him with dread. The old monk loved him, he was sure, and Wend loved the old man.

Sick, suffocating despair spread from the pit of his stomach.

He began to shiver. A bird sang a few detached notes above him. The stream rolled on, indifferent.

He no longer felt the root clutched in his hand. Sleep pulled at his eyes. One small surge in the current could tear him loose.

Maybe I should let go, he thought. He heard roaring in his ears. *I can go to the ocean. See the monks . . . my parents.* For once, he could see the ocean, clearly, just as the monks promised it would be. *I can go there now. Just close my eyes and let go. . . .*

The roaring in his ears got louder. Someone called.

They're there, calling me.

The voice grew louder, closer, more insistent. "What do you want today?" it asked.

Wend opened his eyes. He rubbed away the blur and saw an old man hugging a log, floating downstream toward him.

"What do you want today?" he asked again.

Wend spoke without thinking. "To be warm."

"Then move."

The old man paddled with one hand. He had wiry arms, but they were strong enough to move the log toward Wend.

"How?" asked Wend.

"Swim." The old man smiled. He was close enough that Wend could see white teeth. The left front one was chipped.

"I met you before," said Wend.

"Maybe." The old man was only a few feet away. He held out a hand to Wend. Their fingers almost touched when a wave rolled the log away and the current whisked it downstream.

"More logs coming," the old man cried. "Swim."

Wend watched him disappear around a bend, and then he turned to the falls behind him. A log shot over the edge, sailed through the air, and plunged into the water. It surfaced midstream and the current sped it along. Wend gauged his distance from the log, how fast it was moving, and how long it would take him to swim to it. The log seemed too far away, but another log came tumbling over the waterfall. This one knocked against the rocky side of the gorge opposite to Wend and seesawed down the stream. He waited and watched. The bird above chattered and flew off. A cloud drifted by.

And then a tree trunk sailed over the edge. It seemed to hang in the air like a long wingless bird before plunging nose first into the foam. It surfaced and Wend kicked away from the rock and stroked toward it. He almost despaired of reaching it, but a twist of current rolled the tree toward him and he latched on to the roots. Hand over hand, he pulled himself halfway from the water, and then wrapped his arms around the trunk.

Chapter Five

The Pavilion

The boat's a fish, Wend thought, vaguely aware that he made no sense.

The aroma of roast pig and the laughter of children penetrated the fog in his mind. He rubbed his eyes with cold, stiff fingers, and gazed out.

Half a dozen tents, scattered above a low embankment, were bathed in the afternoon sun. Boys chased each other around a fire. A youth of twelve or thirteen turned a pig on a spit. Three rafts, moored to stakes, drifted languidly. Wend saw no adults.

Two boys played tag along a grassy shore. One froze and pointed at Wend. Then they dashed up the embankment and into one of the tents. A moment later, three older youths streamed out. They bounded down the embankment, leaped onto a raft, and poled toward

Wend. When he was within reach, they plucked him from the tree.

Wend remembered little after that, except sipping hot broth from a bowl, eating a few bites of pork, and the stone-gray eyes of a youth staring at him. Then Wend was taken into a tent, where, curled up in animal skins, warm darkness engulfed him.

Next morning, Wend crawled from the skins and discovered that his robe had been removed. He found a shirt and pants folded nearby. Atop the new clothes sat items he'd kept in his robe pocket: a clay marble that Wonder had given him; and wrapped in a piece of cloth, the center of the wishbone from the magical day with Leena. Along with Leena's bracelet, still around his wrist, these were the only worldly treasures he possessed. Breathing a sigh of relief, he stuffed the marble and bone into the pant pocket and dressed. Soon after, he was taken to a tent and brought before the gray-eyed boy, a youth of fifteen or sixteen. He sat on a stool with one leg flung carelessly before him. His hair was blond, but his brows were dark and cast shadows over his eyes.

He gestured with a pork rib for Wend to sit, then he tore off meat with his teeth and studied Wend while he chewed. "Who came over the cataracts with you?"

"The monks," Wend replied.

"Did they make it?"

Wend's lip trembled. He shook his head.

"Did you see anyone else?"

"An old man on a log."

A smile touched the corners of the youth's mouth. "What's your name?" He was handsome, with delicate lips and a whisper of whiskers on his chin and upper lip. Wend had the sensation that if he touched the boy's face, the skin wouldn't yield and would feel hard as stone.

"Wend."

"I'm Nick Bright. How old are you?"

Wend had to think about that. Not long after joining the monks, he must have passed his birthday. "Six, going on seven."

"Are you hungry?"

Wend nodded. He was given a plate piled with pork and slices of honeyed yam. He hadn't seen this much food in a year.

"Go on, eat," said Nick. "The monks starved you."

Wend wanted to wolf down the whole plate, but he knew his stomach had shrunk, so he ate slowly and sipped from a cup of goat milk.

"Stay with us, and you'll never starve," said Nick.

Wend spent the next days eating and resting. One loop around the encampment gave him the lay of the land. The camp was situated at the base of a hill. A dozen or so tents made from skins were scattered about cooking fires. A few boys played near the fires when the sun rose, but most climbed to the top of the hill and disappeared into a pavilion. Horseradish huddled along the bank, its wrinkled, spear-shaped leaves pointing across the water. A houseboat was moored on the other side of the stream, near a small village. The houses looked deserted.

Wend kept to himself, leaning against a stump. Several boys approached him, but he hugged his knees and looked away. All he could think about was the monks as he watched a cold sun trace across the sky.

Early one morning, Wend walked to the stream. He waded in. The water rose quickly to his neck. He closed his eyes. The current was gentle. It lifted him. He let it take him away. . . .

Yelling and splashing surrounded him. He was dragged from the water and brought to Nick.

"Come here, Wend," Nick said, and tapped his ankles.

Wend sat, leaned against Nick's knees, and felt the boy stroking his hair.

"Where were you going?"

"To be with the monks."

A long pause ensued, during which Nick continued running his fingers through Wend's hair.

"Your parents are dead," Nick said, at last. "And if they're alive, they don't care about you, or they would have found you. The monks, too."

Wend's voice was a strangled whisper. "Don't say that."

"It's true. This is the only safe place for us. The only place where we stay warm and have plenty of food."

"I need to go to the Ocean . . ."

"You can't. Frightening rapids, cascades worse than what destroyed your boat, lie ahead."

"You're lying." Tears rolled down Wend's face.

"It's true. There's only heartbreak ahead."

Wend jerked to his feet, screamed, "I don't believe you. The monks wouldn't lie," and ran from the tent.

The boys foiled several more of Wend's attempts to drift downstream. He gave up trying to leave and was pulled gradually into playing dodge the snake around the cooking fires. Being the youngest, Wend was often the snake. The other boys laughed when he drew near and screamed, "Keep away, keep away, the snake's gonna drag me underwater."

Wend liked the game. The snake was powerful. Chasing the others made him laugh.

Few boys played around the fires, choosing instead to go to the big tent on top of the hill. The boys who went there didn't come out for days. When they finally did, they were glassy-eyed and collapsed on their furs and slept an entire day before they ate.

"What do they do in the Pavilion?" Wend asked Nick one bright afternoon.

Nick smiled. "I'll show you."

The Pavilion was fifteen by thirty feet and made of canvas. Scarlet stripes had been painted on the outside, but the color had faded.

Nick opened the flap and Wend ducked under his arm. It was dim inside, the air damp and thick with sweat. Wend had the sensation that the sides of the tent were expanding, as if the whole tent had inhaled. Compared to the outside, the interior seemed too large.

Boys were sprawled on skins. They seemed half asleep, dreamy expressions on their faces.

"What are they doing?" Wend asked.

"Something greater than you can imagine," Nick replied. "Sit. You'll see."

Wend wanted to leave, to run out of the Pavilion and escape down the hill. He wanted to strip off his clothes, plunge into the stream, and wash the horrible stench of the place off his body, but Nick pressed firmly on his shoulder until he was seated, and then flopped down beside him.

The interior brightened, and not just because Wend's eyes were adjusting. It seemed as if candles were being lit, one by one, but no candle, no lantern could be seen. The grimy sides of the tent changed to the palest blue. The tent seemed to breathe again, expanding out and out. The canvas walls shifted, as if they had dissolved and were now made of mist. Beyond, Wend caught glimpses of sky and trees, and a vast expanse of water.

The Ocean, he thought. Warm peace flowed over him . . .

Nick shook him. "It's time to go."

"I want to stay," Wend complained. "I want to stay with my parents."

"Later," Nick replied. "Not all at once." He picked up Wend and carried him outside. Stars glimmered above. The Boatman, brightest constellation of the night sky, was a pale ghost.

Wend slept until noon. He felt weak, as if he'd swum for miles, but his throat was dry, so he dragged himself from his tent and staggered down to the stream. He drank until his belly was swollen. He turned to walk back to camp when he noticed a canoe being moored beside the rafts. A bear of a man was poised near the prow, holding a coil of rope.

He called to Wend in a voice like gravel. "Snap to, boy. Tie 'er down."

He threw the rope. Wend caught it and tied the canoe to a stake. The man tossed a heavy sack onto the beach and then leaped ashore. He had powerful shoulders and a short, thick neck. A square jaw was covered with sandpaper whiskers, shot with gray. He looked Wend up and down before slinging the sack over one beefy shoulder and stalking off to Nick's tent.

Wend followed the trail back to camp and sat beside one of the cooking fires. He asked Gan, one of the younger boys he played with, who the man was.

"Daggitt," replied Gan, and his ears, smaller than his smallish eyes, seemed to flatten like a cat's.

Wend asked if the houseboat—which was a patchwork of half a dozen boats and sat across the water—belonged to the man.

"It's his," said Gan.

"Why is he here?"

"He brings us stuff."

"In that sack?"

Gan took a pot off of hot coals and poured a cup of coffee. "Did you ever wonder how we got all this?"

Wend had. He'd never seen the boys fish or hunt; never saw them do anything but play or sit in the Pavilion. Except one night, a few days after he'd arrived, he heard whispering outside his tent. He crept to the flap and peeked out. Nick was leading a group of boys down to the rafts, where they pushed off into the stream.

"Daggitt brings us food," said Gan. "Whatever we need."

"Why?"

"We help him. He helps us."

"Is he Nick's dad?"

Gan's face darkened. "He's no one's dad." He threw the rest of his coffee into the fire, where it hissed. "Stay clear of him, if you can."

Daggitt showed up infrequently with his sack, a roll of canvas for tent repairs, or a bundle of clothes. If Wend woke up in the middle of the night and saw the boys slip down to the rafts, the next morning he'd see Daggitt. When he asked Gan what they were doing, Gan replied, "You'll find out soon enough."

Over several months, Wend noticed that different boys went on these nighttime missions. The boys who went were the ones who had been in the Pavilion. And most boys who went into the Pavilion stayed for days, until at last they staggered out.

Seeing them, gaunt and hollow-eyed, made Wend fear the Pavilion. But he felt pulled there too, as if it beckoned. Sometimes, when he passed nearby, he thought he heard laughter, or the strange, haunting song of a flute. Other times, he caught a whiff of fragrance blowing off the hilltop. A scent that reminded him of Leena.

Nick prevented him from satisfying his curiosity. The older boy required Wend to sit at his feet more frequently, where he ran his fingers through Wend's hair and began calling him Puppy.

Wend hated the name, hated Nick's fingers. Over time, fewer boys played by the fires, choosing instead to go up to the Pavilion. Wend decided that the Pavilion was a better place for him too. Better than sitting like a pet at Nick's feet.

One cloudy morning, he rose early and entered the Pavilion. It was crowded with boys, some of whom flopped over each other. Wend stepped around them, heading for a group on the back wall that he'd played with. They appeared to be sleeping, and when he wedged between two of them, only a soft moan escaped their lips.

The stench of stale sweat faded. Time hovered . . .

The tent expanded . . .

The walls melted away . . .

He stood on a towering rock overlooking a tree-carpeted valley. A midday sun in a cloudless sky warmed his brow. The sky shimmered with a rainbow of shifting colors, and distant mountains seemed to float above the horizon.

He was dressed in buckskins. A falcon stood on his shoulder. Stripes of orange and black war paint glistened on his arms. He touched his face, and his fingertip came away black.

A knife hung from a leather belt at his hip. He pulled it from the sheath and gasped. The knife was as translucent as crystal. He tested the edge. *Sharper than knives on the stream,* he thought in wonder.

The falcon called sharply. Wend followed the bird's gaze. Gan and three boys Wend had played with were trotting along a trail below.

Wend called to them.

"Come on, Wend!" cried Gan. "We're fighting the Unnug tribe."

The falcon took off and circled above while Wend climbed down the rock.

"Why are we fighting?" Wend asked when he'd joined them.

"They stole the master knife from us." Gan grinned, warping the red and blue circles painted on his face. "We're gettin' it back. Weapons drawn, men. They might ambush us."

They drew their knives, and Gan led them into a stand of pines, where they dropped behind a fallen tree.

"They're camped in a clearing beyond those trees," he said. "Let's surround 'em. Don't attack until you hear me whoop."

The boys crept forward, then took off, darting from tree to tree, until they reached the perimeter of the clearing.

This is play, isn't it? Wend thought. *Like fighting pirates with Leena.* But he and Leena had fought with sticks. Now he wore buckskin and warpaint and held a strange knife. He held his breath and peeked around the trunk. The clearing was empty of tents, cooking fire, pots. And enemy. He exhaled in relief.

The Stream

Gan signaled them to divide and take up positions. Wend took off, running low to the ground. He dropped behind a rock and waited. The only sounds were a tree creaking in the wind and the occasional piping of a titmouse. Then Gan whooped. A moment later, he charged into the clearing from the rear. Wend sprang up and dashed into the clearing, brandishing his knife. The other boys streaked in. The glade rang with their battle cries. They dueled, swiping, stabbing, and lunging at air.

"Watch out, Wend," cried Gan. "There's one behind you!"

Wend whirled and parried. "Coward. Take that." The knife whistled as he thrust. His laughter lifted to the tops of the trees.

"To their lodge, men," Gan shouted. "Get the master knife."

They rushed toward a massive oak. Eight feet of the trunk leaned to the right. The rest had splintered and fallen, the fanning branches forming a shady enclosure. The boys ducked inside.

"Wend, grab the knife!" said Gan. "We'll hold them off."

"Where is it?"

Gan pointed to a rotten hole in the trunk.

Wend darted to the hole, grabbed the pretend knife, and waved it, triumphantly. "Got it."

"Now our power is tenfold," Gan cried. "No one can stand in our way. To our stronghold!"

They retreated to the towering rock where Wend had first stood and seated themselves in a circle at the top.

"Put the knife in the middle," said Gan.

Wend extended his arm. A crystal knife materialized in his hand. The blade began to glow.

Chapter Six

Purlo

Wend couldn't say whether he'd spent hours or days in the Pavilion. When he staggered out, night enveloped the camp in darkness. He was thirsty and hungry, but far too tired to do anything but pass out in his tent. When he awoke, the rising moon seemed narrower than it had been. He guessed he'd slept two days.

The world was pale and drab, as if it had faded. The change frightened him, but that was small compared to the ravenous hunger gnawing his stomach. He doddered down to one of the cooking fires, where he found roast deer, still steaming on the spit. He cut off a chunk and wolfed it down, followed by a long drink from a water skin.

He rested and ate, rested and ate, for the next few hours.

At one point, Nick stopped by the fire to eat and glanced at him disapprovingly. "I want my puppy." But he left Wend alone, and Wend napped and ate and crawled back to his tent to sleep through the night.

The next morning, the world still seemed pale. He marched down to the stream and threw himself in. The water was cold and bracing, but it felt good. He stayed submerged until the need for air sent him sputtering to the surface. When he looked down at the water, he didn't recognize the boy reflected back. The cheeks were so drawn that the bones protruded. The eyes were sunken and vacant.

Most frightening was the world . . . Color had been stripped from tree and sky. A blue jay, landing on the shore to snatch a worm from the mud, was as brown as dead leaves.

Wend felt a sudden urge to scrub his face and body. He scrubbed until his skin was raw, and then he floated on his back, eyes closed, and let the current flow by . . .

When he opened his eyes at last, the world sang with color.

In his tent that night, Wend whispered to Gan, "Was it real?"

Gan groaned. "Was what real?"

"The valley. Our buckskins."

"Does it matter?"

The Stream

Wend lay on his side with his head propped in his hand. "Maybe we are in the Pavilion the whole time and only think we left."

"Who cares, as long as you're having fun."

"We pretended there was a master knife, and then it appeared in my hand."

"It was there all along."

Wend sat up. "You saw it? Before?"

In the shadows, Gan's smallish eyes seemed like the pale disks of a bird. "Go to sleep. You ask too many questions."

But Wend couldn't sleep. Questions tumbled into his mind. Did Gan see the enemy encampment? Did he see enemies? The implications frightened Wend, and he was afraid to ask.

His instincts told him that the Pavilion was dangerous. That it drew you in, deeper and deeper, until you never wanted to leave.

Wend swore he wouldn't go back, but the lure was too great. He returned, day after day, to new adventures in new lands. With bows and arrows—*magic* bows and arrows that could shoot seven leagues and never miss—he and his comrades battled blue-skinned giants. They fought with poison darts against lizard monsters whose teeth cut like knives. And found treasure in a chamber filled with gold and glittering gemstones.

Wend was with whoever was in the Pavilion at the time, but sometimes he roamed alone, traveling through strange cities made of quartz, villages built high in the trees, and towns where statues talked and strode on paths as wide as a river. He explored lands where boats lifted off the stream and, catching the wind in their sails, flew over forests and mountains. He discovered a house, larger than a hill, whose spires seemed to scrape a sky as shiny as polished metal. In a great hall inside, where a choir of birds sang in human voices, Wend found a banquet offering an endless supply of food and drink unlike any he had tasted.

Each time he left the Pavilion, he felt weaker, more famished. And something new: nausea and dizziness gripped him, and he felt as sick as he had after eating poison mushrooms. Most painful was what happened to the world, which faded more and more into a pale ghost. Longer baths in the stream were required to bring color and vibrancy back to the world.

He couldn't say whether he was far from the ocean, like the shaggy woodchopper who couldn't see him, but he felt far from the stream, and that entering the Pavilion betrayed the monks and his parents. He swore he'd never set foot there again.

He always did, and would have gone more, but Nick often caught him before he could go up the hill and had him sit at his feet.

"You don't go up to the Pavilion much," Wend said one day.

"I've got something better." Nick tapped a jug on a table beside him. "Nummrak."

He uncorked the jug and let Wend sniff it. The scent was strong and made Wend's eyes burn. Nick laughed. Raising the jug to his lips, he took a long swig.

"Much better," he said, wiping his mouth on his sleeve. "This'll put hair on your chest, Puppy."

Wend hated the name. He hated sitting at Nick's feet, hated Nick's fingers in his hair. He was about to complain when a new boy was brought into the tent. He was ten or eleven, tall for his age, and had straight, almost white hair. A nasty sunburn peeled on his nose and cheeks.

Nick asked the same questions he'd asked Wend: the boy's name, who he came over the cataracts with, whether he was alone. The boy's name was Purlo. Two boats had gone over the cataracts, his parents' and his uncle's. His parents had perished. He thought his uncle, aunt, and cousins had survived.

"Why?" asked Nick.

"Their boat didn't capsize until they went over the last fall. I saw them swim away."

Nick's eyes narrowed. "Did they see you?"

Purlo fought back tears. "I don't think so. I've got to go to them. They'll be rebuilding their boat."

One of Nick's deputies brought in duck, pulled dripping from the spit. The aroma made Wend's mouth water.

"Hungry?" Nick asked.

Purlo gazed longingly at the food but hesitated.

"Don't be bashful," said Nick. "We've got plenty."

"Maybe a little," said Purlo. "Then I've got to get going." He sat cross-legged and began devouring breast meat.

"Bring him goat milk, Puppy."

Wend was happy to get Nick's fingers out of his hair. He ducked out of the tent, fetched a pitcher of milk, and set it beside Purlo. Then he faded to a corner of the tent, hoping Nick wouldn't notice him.

Propping his head in his hand, Nick studied Purlo. "Your uncle may not have made it," Nick said.

Purlo took a long drink from the pitcher. "He made it. He's tough as gnarled oak, and floats like it too. They all are. My aunt, my cousins. I saw them swimming toward broken pieces of their boat."

Nick shook his head. "There are frightening rapids ahead, and cascades worse than what destroyed your boat. No one survives those."

"Maybe, but he'll build a new one. He works when he's sad."

"There's nowhere to build a boat."

Purlo stared at Nick and seemed to be gauging Nick's honesty. "There is. The river splits upstream. I fought it, but the current took me down this way. Last I saw my uncle and his family, they were carried the other way."

"You were dreaming."

"I saw it."

Wend felt a thrill go through him. If the stream split, as Purlo said, it might explain the nighttime missions, and where all the food was coming from. Maybe there was a community of people on the other strand of the river. Wend had seen these before, places where people stopped and lived for a time.

"The stream is death," Nick said bitterly. "Anyone who goes on it dies. You're safe here."

Purlo's lip trembled, and tears filled his eyes. "My uncle thinks I'm dead. It's tearing him up. I've got to get to him so he knows I'm all right."

"Sure you do." Nick's voice was smooth, but it had an edge to it, like a broken piece of fine porcelain. "But you need rest." He spotted Wend squatting in a shadow. "Puppy, take him to the Pavilion. He can rest there."

Wend stepped from the shadow and took Purlo's arm. "It's all right. Take a short nap. I'll wake you."

Purlo nodded and allowed Wend to lead him from the tent. They started up the hill toward the Pavilion.

"Did the stream really split?" Wend asked.

"It did. I pulled out of the water and climbed a hill to see where my uncle might have gone. There's a maze of tributaries over there, feeding into the other branch of the stream. I tried swimming across this branch, hoping to find my uncle, but the current was too strong and took me here."

"I wish you'd found him."

"Me too, but I will. He can't be far."

Wend glanced behind to see if they were being watched. No one left or entered Nick's tent. A few boys played around one of the cooking fires.

"Don't go in the Pavilion," said Wend. "It's a trick. You won't want to leave."

Purlo gazed up at the Pavilion. Its canvas fluttered in the wind. "It's just a tent."

"No. It isn't. You've got to run. Get away from this place."

"They'll see me."

"Follow me," said Wend.

They reached the top of the hill. Wend surveyed the encampment. No one was watching them. A few more steps and they'd be out of sight. He took Purlo around the back of the Pavilion, where a shadow of a path led down the other side of the hill to a dense cluster of box elders.

"Hide in those trees until dark. Then run for it."

"Won't he look for me before then?"

"No, if you'd gone into the Pavilion, you'd be there until tonight."

"What about you?"

"If I don't go back to him, he'll think I went into the Pavilion. He'll come looking for me, and he'll see you're not there. I'll bring you a blanket later. Wait until the camp is dark. Then slip down to the stream and take one of the rafts."

"What good will that do? You can't go upstream."

"Cross to the other side of the river. There's a deserted village there, and a hill behind it. Maybe you'll find the tributaries behind the hill."

Purlo gripped Wend's hands. "Come with me. My uncle will take you in."

Wend wavered. He hadn't thought about leaving since his early attempts to return to the ocean. But was it safe to go? Nick said there were dangers ahead — rapids and waterfalls worse than any Wend had seen. But how could Nick know? Who could come back to tell him? No one travels upstream.

Purlo dropped Wend's hands and pointed emphatically to the Pavilion. "What about that?"

Purlo was right. The biggest argument for leaving was the Pavilion. Wend felt it calling. If it were a dark hole, he could turn his back, but it was a bright, glittering thing that ensnared him with his own dreams. Sometimes he wondered if it might take him so far away that he would never come back.

"If it's not safe for me, then it's not safe for you," said Purlo.

Wend wavered, like a sail boom that could flop either way, waiting for a puff of wind to decide its fate. He realized that his hand was in his pocket, and he was turning in his fingers the tip of the wishbone Leena had given him.

Leena would be courageous. She swam dangerous waters just for the fun of it. He could almost hear her voice in his head: "Come on, Wend. Let's see the tributaries!"

"Okay," said Wend. "I'll come when it's dark. Better get going. I've got to get back."

Wend watched Purlo trot down the path and disappear into the trees. Then Wend turned and followed the trail back to camp. The last place he wanted to go was Nick's tent, but he pushed past the flap and stepped inside. Daggitt was there with a haunch of deer and a large jug, like the one Nick had shown Wend earlier. Daggitt's sack was at his feet, and he was pulling a knife from it.

Nick glanced at Wend as he entered and then returned his attention to Daggitt, who pulled a pot from the sack. Wend slipped out of the tent. From past experience, he knew that Daggitt would be with Nick for some time.

He ran to the tent of one of the boys who he'd seen go into the Pavilion that morning. A boy who spent days there. Wend peered into the tent. It was empty. He looked around to make sure he wasn't watched, and then he sneaked into the tent and rolled up the boy's furs. With the furs under one arm, he returned to the tent flap and peeked out. Other than the boys playing around the fire, the camp was deserted. No one had emerged from Nick's tent.

Wend walked casually to his own tent, where he buried the boy's furs under his own.

Tendrils of fog snaked through the trees. The moon had set. The sun wouldn't rise for four more hours.

Wend and Purlo left the trees. Circling around the base of the hill, they crept toward camp from the side. Fog cloaked the tents. Faint glowing marked the cooking fires. The only sound was the murmuring of the stream.

They skirted the camp. When they came to the water, Purlo slipped aboard the first raft. Wend untied the mooring line. Straddling the raft and the shore, he launched them with a push of his foot and stepped aboard.

Purlo worked the pole with strong, steady strokes. Wend took the paddle and dipped it silently.

Fog rose from the water, as if the stream had exhaled. The camp and trees faded into dreamy silhouettes. Ahead, Daggitt's boat and the deserted village were hidden behind a wall of mist.

Wend tingled with nervous excitement. The Pavilion seemed far away, and like the cobwebs of a nightmare, it was dissolving.

The fog bank masked their escape. No one would know they were gone unless someone saw the missing raft. And no one would. The nighttime missions never started this late.

The danger was running into Daggitt's boat. Or getting swept downstream; they would never be able to return and find Purlo's uncle.

"The current's strong," Wend whispered. "More to your left, or we'll miss the village."

They put their backs into it. Beyond an occasional prompt from Wend to shift course, neither boy spoke.

Dark smudges melted from the fog, blurry impressions of the village, trees, and the hill beyond. Wend had the sensation that he was passing into another world. He wondered what life would be like with Purlo's uncle and aunt.

"They'll love you like their own," Purlo had said, while they'd waited in the trees for night to deepen. "My cousin will be your brother."

"They're kind folks."

"We're all one family. That's what my dad used to say . . ." Purlo stifled a sob.

Wend had put his arm around the boy's shoulders. "He was wise."

The Stream

That seemed too much for Purlo. He'd leaned against Wend and cried a long time.

"What happened to your parents?" Purlo asked, wiping his eyes at last.

"They died in a storm."

"Do you still miss them?"

"Every day. When I was with the monks, they said my parents were waiting for me in the Great Ocean."

"Do you believe that?"

"Sometimes. Do you?"

"I want to. My dad said there's only the stream. One long strand that keeps going forever."

"Then why are we here?" Wend had asked.

"To hold onto each other."

The village loomed. A hundred yards downstream, Daggitt's boat was a ghost in the fog. No light came from the windows.

They steered the raft to the remains of a dock and tied it to an old post that had been one of the support pillars.

Purlo nodded toward the pillars, which leaned like broken tree stumps. "Must have been some flood," he muttered.

They stepped into the village, making no more sound than the wind. The doorways and windows of the houses were black, empty.

"I wonder why they left," whispered Wend.

"No one stays in a village long," Purlo replied. "They bide awhile, then move on."

The villagers must have taken almost everything with them, or else others coming along had picked the homes clean. No curtains, paintings, or rugs adorned the interiors; no cooking pots or tools waited for busy hands. Only a few lonely sticks of furniture remained.

If gardens had once grown between the huts, they were now consumed by grass and shrubs native to the stream.

The boys followed a path out of the village. Ahead, shrouded in fog, a solitary cabin stood at the base of the hill. As the boys approached, a hulking form materialized from the mist. At first, Wend thought it was a bear, but as the figure stepped forward it resolved into Daggitt. A rope swung from his right hand. His eyes—flat, pale disks beneath the shadow of his brow—locked onto Wend.

Chapter Seven

Dark Business

"Run!" Wend screamed.

He shoved Purlo to the left to get him going, and then dashed to the right and back toward the village. If Purlo could get away, perhaps Wend could sneak past Daggitt later.

Wend darted behind one of the houses and listened. He heard no sound of pursuit. Slipping from house to house, he made his way to the other side of the village and crept into one of the houses. It was empty save for a broken stool, a wooden table, and years of dust.

Peeking from a back window, he watched the trail leading up the hill. No one was on it. Purlo could have run for the trees to the left of the solitary cabin, or he could have retreated to this side of the village.

A. R. Silverberry

Wend smiled in grim satisfaction. Daggitt couldn't be in two places at once. Eventually, he'd go across the river, rouse the boys, and bring back a search party. By that time, Wend and Purlo would be over the hill. Purlo would be moving and hiding, but he'd also be looking for Wend. And they both would be searching for Purlo's uncle.

Chances were good they'd find each other.

Wend watched, waited, listened. Black night bled into gray.

The fog would lift. At some point he had to risk crossing the open space to go up the trail past the cabin or lose himself in the trees on either side.

A strange feeling rooted him where he stood. If he left, he would be abandoning Purlo. Shaking off the feeling, he made his way back to the other side of the village until he could peer from the side of the last house to the trail beyond.

Daggitt stood near the solitary cabin holding one end of the rope. The other end was tied around Purlo's arms, securing them to his sides. Purlo breathed heavily, as if trying to catch his breath.

"Come out," Daggitt yelled, "or I'll break his foot."

Wend stepped from behind the house. "Don't hurt him."

Purlo struggled at his bonds. "Run, Wend."

Daggitt picked up a stone the size of a small melon. "I'll smash his foot. I swear it."

"It's okay, I'm coming." Wend gauged his chances. He could stumble and fall right before reaching Daggitt, and then rise with a handful of dirt and throw it in the man's face. If Daggitt clutched at his eyes, he might drop the rope. Wend and Purlo could run for it.

How many seconds would elapse before Daggitt pursued them? His legs were longer. Purlo wouldn't be able to run quickly with the rope pinning his arms.

Daggitt would go for him first and crush his foot. Wend couldn't risk that.

Wend was about ten feet away. "He's not like the other boys. He's got an uncle, over by the tributaries."

"He's got no one but me now."

"Why can't we leave?"

"You've eaten my food. Used my plates. Drank out of my cups." Face dark, eyes inflamed, Daggitt spat. "Pay the price, or pay the devil."

The sun rose, cold and pale behind an overcast sky.

Wend and Purlo had spent a restless night tied to one of the awning poles on Daggitt's houseboat.

The rope bit into Wend's wrists. With his arms pulled behind and tied around the pole, his shoulders and back were soon cramping.

The boys tested the strength of the knots but gave up trying to escape when the skin on their arms chafed raw. Daggitt knew his way around ropes.

He was in the cabin now, snoring.

A. R. Silverberry

The air smelled of rain. The first big drops hit the awning and the deck late morning. Only then did Daggitt begin banging around inside the cabin. He emerged an hour later, jug in hand. Without a glance at Purlo or Wend, he leaped off the boat and staggered into the village.

He returned midafternoon, threw the boys into the canoe, crossed the stream, and dragged Wend and Purlo into Nick's tent, where they were tossed on the ground.

"Next time, I'll snap their necks," Daggitt said to Nick. He started to leave but turned at the tent flap. "We go tonight. There's rare pickings."

After Daggitt left, Nick rested his chin in one hand and stared at Wend. "It's time you learn how things work."

Wend rose and dusted himself off. "Why can't we leave?"

"I told you, it's not safe."

"We'll take our chances."

"It doesn't work like that. We took you in. Gave you food and a place to sleep. Now you have to do your part." Nick turned to two of his deputies. "Take Purlo to the Pavilion. Make sure he stays. Sit on him if you have to."

"No," Wend cried. "He didn't do anything. He just wants to be with his uncle." He watched in dismay as Purlo was dragged from the tent.

The Stream

Wend checked the urge to run. Two more of Nick's henchman were outside the tent. Even if Wend got past them, Daggitt probably hadn't launched his canoe yet.

"You've got fight in you." Nick twisted a lock of his hair into a hook that framed one eye. "Bring that tonight."

Behind clouds, the moon was a fleeting specter, barely illuminating the path that wound upward through oaks and alders. The deserted village lay behind, buried in the night. Ahead, Daggitt and Nick were nothing more than shadows.

Gan licked his lips. His glance darted repeatedly from Daggitt to the trees on either side, as if he might run at any moment.

"Are you all right?" Wend whispered.

Gan put a finger to his lips to signal quiet. He smiled, but his face was ashen.

A few teasing drops threatened rain as they plodded up the trail. A chill wind greeted them when they reached the summit.

Wend stopped short and gasped, for he was like a fish that leaps from water for the first time and catches a glimpse of the wider world. Row upon row of silhouetted hills stretched to distant mountains. Then the clouds parted and moonlight struck the tributaries, which branched and branched like a colossal tree and shone like molten silver. They converged on a single point, beyond which a mighty river snaked through forestland until it faded in mist.

The cold forgotten, he could have lingered, but like that fish, his time on the summit was all too brief; the journey continued and he plunged back into the woods. The hoot of an owl was the only sound as they passed.

Wend was uncertain what their mission was. One thing was clear. If Daggitt had left boats or rafts, they could cut across several of the tributaries. Forests like this would have plenty of food, and Wend guessed that communities of stream people had congregated along the inlets and islands, some building new boats, others ready to continue their journey downstream.

As the trail leveled near the bottom of the hill, perspiration sprang to Gan's forehead. He stopped and bent over. Goose and Clod, two of Nick's deputies bringing up the rear, prodded him on.

"He needs water," said Wend. "He's got the ague."

Goose looked at Clod and laughed. "More like yellow feet." But he let Gan sip from a waterskin.

When they neared the shore, Daggitt signaled them to slow. He glanced back at Gan and swore. "Deal with it, Nicky."

Scowling, Nick doubled back. "What's the problem, Gan?"

Gan jerked in short breaths, not for air, but to fight back tears. "I can't do it, Nick."

"That's okay," Nick replied smoothly. "We'll just take a break from the Pavilion."

Blood drained from Gan's face.

"You can wait for us here," said Nick. "Clod, make sure Gan doesn't go into the Pavilion when we get back."

"What do you think?" asked Clod. "Two weeks?"

"Better make it three." Nick smiled.

"No . . ." Gan's voice was strangled.

"Well, what's it gonna be?" Nick asked.

Gan wiped his brow. "I'll be okay, Nick, I promise."

Nick clapped him on the back. "Good man. You'll harden up, you'll see."

Daggitt stopped them when they reached the trees along the shore. A light rain fell, disturbing the surface of the stream, which wound around half a dozen islands.

Leading them off the trail, Daggitt came to a pile of fallen branches, thick with leaves. He and Nick pulled away the branches to reveal two canoes. With two people on each end, they carried the canoes to the water. The party divided; Wend, Gan, Nick, and Daggitt launched the lead boat.

As they glided along, Wend saw a half-finished boat propped up on the shore of the largest island. A small tent crouched nearby, suggesting only one boat maker lived there.

Daggitt guided the canoes straight across the channel. When they arrived at the opposite shore, they pulled the canoes onto a sandy spit and hiked over a short hill until they met another channel. Daggitt had two rafts hidden. These were launched, and soon they were gliding between two islands.

On the opposite shore of the channel, hidden behind one of the islands, a boat was moored. Daggitt steered them to it, and when the rafts were alongside, he cocked his head and listened. The windows were dark. The only sound came from the occasional groan of the boat's prow line, which was tied to a large overhanging oak.

Wend realized with a strangling pang what they were doing, and who they were.

"River pirates—" he whispered. "We can't. It's stealing."

Nick clamped his hand over Wend's mouth.

Daggitt hissed, "Keep your whelp quiet, Nick, or I'll put him out of his misery."

Under his breath, Nick spoke into Wend's ear, "You'll be quiet?"

Wend nodded, and Nick released him.

Daggitt signaled Nick, Gan, and three boys from the other raft. The boys rose. Nick laced his fingers and boosted Gan onto the boat.

"Stay here," Nick whispered to Wend. "Make sure the raft doesn't drift."

The Stream

Nick pulled himself silently onto the boat. Daggitt followed, drawing a knife from his belt when he was on board.

Wend could see little of what they did, but Nick soon returned to the raft, and Daggitt and Gan passed baskets and sacks down to him. When both rafts were filled with spoils, the boys returned and tied the goods down.

Something creaked, perhaps a cabin door. Silence followed. A strangled cry trailed off into a gurgle. Wend's mind raced. He looked wildly about. No boats were in sight. No lanterns flared.

Heavy footsteps drew closer to the rail. Daggitt loomed on the edge of the deck, his blade dripping red.

By the time Wend got back to camp, every muscle ached. He gave it no mind; deeper pain stabbed him. He wanted to pace, despite sore feet, but Goose and Clod were watching him. He slipped into his tent and sat on his bed furs. Gan entered a moment later, slipped under his furs, and pulled them over his head. They hadn't spoken on the way back. Judging by Gan's face, he wouldn't talk for a while.

Wend understood that. Numbness, then waves of nausea left him soaked with sweat. He held his stomach, the pain no less than if a knife were twisting inside. How he could have been part of it? Why hadn't he warned the man in the boat?

Neither cowardice nor self-preservation had stopped him, despite Daggitt's threat to snap his neck. One thought had filled his mind. He had to help Purlo.

The Pavilion hadn't tainted Purlo. He was good and had a family to go to who loved him. Wend didn't know what he could do for the other boys. Perhaps the Pavilion had sucked them in too deep. But he could do something for Purlo.

He could help him escape.

But how? Wend could try to connect with Purlo after he left the Pavilion, but Nick would be watching for that.

A better plan was to sneak into the Pavilion . . .

After a restless sleep, Wend rose late in the afternoon and looked for Purlo. He didn't see him in any of the tents or near the cooking fire. That meant that Purlo was still in the Pavilion, either forgotten, or more sinister, being allowed to sink into a dreamy abyss from which he would never return.

Wend had to get to him soon, but as he'd feared, Goose and Clod watched him. They couldn't forever.

Daggitt brought the spoils that evening. He didn't stay long. Goose and Clod joined Nick in his tent, and soon nummrak-slurred singing and laughter peppered the night. A few hours later, Goose and Clod staggered to their tents.

The Stream

When the camp was quiet, Wend slipped up the hill and into the Pavilion. Purlo was on the far end, propped against a tent pole. His eyes were lidded, his mouth half open, his lips cracked.

No one guarded him. Wend guessed that the deputies had left as soon as they saw Purlo sucked into a dream. Older boys took longer to nod out.

Wend would go down fast. He had to be quick, or the Pavilion would take him.

Squatting, he shook Purlo's foot but got no response. Wend reached for Purlo's hands and yanked. Still nothing.

Wend felt the Pavilion breathe . . . in and out, and out . . .

"Purlo," Wend whispered sharply in his friend's ear, so he didn't disturb the others. Some older boys who might be allied with Nick lay scattered about.

A sharp pinch on Purlo's arm elicited a soft moan, and he tried to roll onto his side.

. . . in and out, and out . . .

Wend drew from his pocket a chunk of horseradish root that he had peeled. He rubbed the root beneath Purlo's eyes. Breaking off a piece, he put it on the boy's tongue —

. . . a hundred candles blazing . . . canvas walls fading to blue . . .

— Wend grabbed both shoulders and shook his friend for all he was worth.

Purlo spit out the horseradish. His eyes fluttered open. He rubbed them and looked around, dazed.

Wend grabbed his hands and yanked. "Come on. We've got to get out of here."

Purlo rose, unsteady on his feet. With Wend supporting him, they stepped around the sleeping boys and out into the night.

Wend took Purlo to the cluster of trees where they'd met, three nights ago. Purlo took a long pull from a waterskin and devoured a slab of deer meat. When he was strong enough, they slipped down to the stream and launched one of the rafts.

Drizzle pulled a gauzy veil over the camp behind and the village ahead. It didn't hide them as the fog had, but Wend hoped it would be enough.

Purlo worked the pole. "I saw my parents."

"No. It wasn't real."

"How do we keep Daggitt from catching us again?"

"We'll try to land near his boat. He'd never think we'd go there."

A gossamer net of droplets glistened on Purlo's hair. "If we miss the spot, we'll end up downstream. I'll never see my family."

"I know."

As if to emphasize Purlo's point, the raft dipped into a rush of current and began to turn. Wend put his back into paddling until they were in calmer water.

"We'll split up when we land," said Wend. "Don't take the trail. We'll head up the hill from different sides and cut through the trees."

"Where do we meet?"

"At the summit."

Purlo thrust his pole into the stream, as if he wanted to speed up their journey. Daggitt's boat was moored near a treelined inlet. At the top end of the inlet was a small clearing with a crude, broken-down fence at the waterline.

The raft was on course to land above Daggitt's boat. The current was calm now. They could let the raft drift until they were adjacent to the fence, which they could reach with a dozen easy strokes. Then they could disappear into the trees.

Still, Wend had misgivings. The only work Daggitt knew was dark work. He sucked on others like a mosquito. Mosquitoes weren't easy to wave away.

"Purlo? If something goes wrong, if we get separated, we need a signal."

The current was almost motionless. Purlo leaned on the pole and rested. "What are you thinking?"

Wend pulled his oar from the water and set it down. He opened a gunnysack he had filled with clothes and food and stashed aboard the raft. Taking a bright red bandanna from the sack, he held it up. "If we get caught, I'll tie this where you'll see it. That'll mean that the boys are on a mission and it's safe for you to run for it."

"What about you?"

"I'll try to meet up with you later, but don't wait for me. If we don't make it this time, just go. Get out of here."

"I won't leave you."

"You don't understand. They're river pirates. They kill people."

They let the raft drift. Daggitt's boat loomed. The awning fluttered with a breath of wind and then sat still.

Wend took up his paddle and dipped it as quietly as he could. Drizzle disturbed the surface of the water. The boat's reflection was a murky shadow.

As they neared the fence, Purlo reached for one of the posts and pulled them in. Wend tied the raft to a post, and then both boys climbed over the fence.

The rope tying Daggitt's boat to shore groaned. Wend glanced at the cabin windows. They were black, empty. He held his breath, but no lantern was lit.

The boys stepped lightly across the clearing. They were five feet from the perimeter when Wend heard something large crashing through the foliage. A moment later, Daggitt burst from the trees.

Chapter Eight

Daggitt

Daggitt tied Wend and Purlo to the awning pole and retired to the cabin for the night. The awning gave little protection. Rain blew in flurries, the kind of rain that soaks you in minutes and makes you long for a fire and a tent.

A puddle grew beneath them. They huddled as best they could for warmth.

"I'm never going to see my uncle," Purlo said in a strained whisper.

"You will," replied Wend.

Purlo began to cry softly. "What kind of place is this . . ."

They spoke little after that. Despite the rain, Wend fell asleep from exhaustion.

He awoke at dawn. The rain had stopped. Drops still fell from the awning and smacked onto the deck. He shivered.

Daggitt rose late in the morning and untied Purlo from the pole. His hands were retied behind his back, and another rope was looped around his neck. Daggitt kept the end of the neck rope tight in one hand.

"What about me?" asked Wend.

"You're staying," said Daggitt.

Desperation rose inside Wend. "Why?"

Daggitt brought his face inches from Wend's. His breath smelled like rotten fish and nummrak. "Time to pay the devil."

Daggitt tossed Purlo into the canoe. Wend watched in dismay as Daggitt paddled across the stream to the boys' camp. Twenty minutes later, he returned and untied Wend.

"If you care about your friend, don't think about running," said Daggitt.

Wend rubbed his wrists. "Why are you keeping me?"

"I've been watching you. You're small, but you make trouble." He brought his face an inch from Wend's. "I don't like trouble." He waved his arm, indicating the boat. "Clean it, top to bottom. Do you cook?"

"A little."

"Better learn, better be good." He went into the cabin. A moment later he emerged with a nummrak jug, leaped ashore, and disappeared into the trees across the clearing.

Wend's heart pounded so hard it drummed in his ears. *Go! Get out of here!* he thought. *Before he comes back!*

But he couldn't run. Something terrible would happen to Purlo.

A gust of wind shook the leaves. He fought the urge to sink to his feet and cry. He wandered aimlessly about the boat, only half seeing it. His mind raced back to Daggitt.

How long will he keep me? How will he treat me? Will I be beaten?

The only thing he knew for certain was that his life had taken a terrible turn. Daggitt was strong, harsh, and on the edge of exploding like a winter storm.

Wend clutched the boat rail and took deep breaths until the drumming in his ears subsided.

Better start cleaning.

When he entered the cabin, Wend realized cleaning would take days. The bed furs had been flung so haphazardly it appeared that a body was twisted inside them. Dirty clothes were piled in a corner and thrown over a chair. Empty nummrak jugs littered the floor. The table and floor were strewn with bits of moldy flatbread, dried fish, and duck bones.

The cabin reeked of rotting food and stale sweat. Wend opened the windows and began to clean. Working helped him pull his thoughts together and consider his options.

Two attempts to get by Daggitt had failed. Now he would be on full alert. Wend could jump into a canoe and run downstream. Daggitt might follow, but he'd be leaving a sweet deal. Boys desperate for the Pavilion did his bidding. A maze of tributaries held survivors from the cataracts. A slit throat in the night didn't talk the next day. No one would trace piracy back here. The few poor souls coming down this channel, if they weren't children, were told to move on. Or killed.

It stopped raining. Wend brought the bed furs topside and hung them to air on the awning crossbeam. He collected the dirty clothes and piled them on the deck.

He mustn't show weakness. If Daggitt perceived weakness, he would become vicious.

With a broom, Wend sent crumbs and bones flying from the table. He swept the floor clean and buried the garbage in a corner of the clearing. He found a pail and a brush beneath a tangle of old rope. After filling the pail with stream water, he scrubbed grease and nummrak stains from the table, and began working on the floor.

His only option, he told himself, was to be patient, wait until Daggitt and Nick went on a raid, and then tie the bandanna somewhere so Purlo knew it was safe to run. If Purlo crossed the stream, he and Wend would flee.

Daggitt returned at sundown, threw a dressed duck at Wend's feet, and growled, "Cook it."

Wend already had a fire going in the clearing, and soon the duck was sizzling over flames. Daggitt walked around the boat and disappeared into the cabin.

When the duck was cooked, Wend placed it on a plate and carried it to Daggitt's table, where the man was sharpening a hunting knife.

"You didn't finish cleaning," Daggitt said without looking up from his work.

"You live like a pig," Wend said boldly. "No one could clean it in less than three days."

Wend held his breath, ready to dodge a blow. Daggitt's eyes hardened a moment, but then he grunted and cut a chunk of duck for his plate.

The aroma of the duck was maddening. Wend hadn't eaten since before crossing the stream with Purlo, and his stomach rumbled. He was uncertain if he was allowed to partake. Daggitt made no move to share.

What do I have to lose? Wend asked himself. He pulled up a chair and reached for a duck leg.

Daggitt slapped Wend's hand aside. "I didn't say you get any."

"I cooked it. I get to eat it." Wend reached for the leg and this time Daggitt let him take it.

Daggitt speared a piece of duck with his knife. He ate the meat off the blade and studied Wend while he chewed. "I want this boat cleaned by tomorrow night," he said.

Wend stared back, hoping he looked calmer than he felt. "It'll take all day just to wash your clothes."

Daggitt shoved back his chair, rose, and grabbed his nummrak jug. "Don't push it, kid." He strode from the cabin.

There wasn't much left of the duck. Wend picked what he could from the bones, saved a wing tip for an offering to the stream, and left the cabin. Daggitt was leaning against the fence near the prow, smoking a pipe.

Wend knelt by the edge of the boat. He was about to drop the wing into the water when Daggitt asked, "What're you doing?"

"The stream brings gifts. I'm returning mine."

"Come here."

Wend approached. When he was within reach, Daggitt backhanded him. "That's the only gift you'll get."

Wend rose early. He took the dirty clothes to the stream and began scrubbing them over rocks. He had a good view of the encampment and could watch the comings and goings of the boys. Gan played briefly by the fire and then went up the hill to the Pavilion. Goose and Clod went into Nick's tent midmorning. Purlo wasn't in sight.

After washing the clothes, Wend untangled an old rope and strung it between two trees in the clearing. Then he hung the clothes to dry.

At noon, Daggitt emerged from the cabin eating a piece of flatbread and crossed to the clearing.

"Light the fire," he said.

Wend used flint he had found in one of the abandoned houses to start the fire. When it crackled, Daggitt stood by the flames and spread his hands to warm them.

A cat, no older than five months, stepped from the foliage at the edge of the clearing. One eye was almost closed from a slash across the left side of his face. Meowing, it made a beeline for Wend and Daggitt. Daggitt picked up a stone and threw it, chasing the cat back into the bushes.

"No," Wend cried. "He likes us."

"He's begging and he's useless."

"But we can help."

"But I won't. You think the stream brings gifts? His was a slash across the eye."

"He just needs a friend."

"He won't find one here." Daggitt stalked off to the village.

Wend spent the rest of the day scrubbing the deck. He watched the boys' camp while he worked, hoping to catch a glance of Purlo, but didn't see him. Were they guarding him? Or had they dragged him back to the Pavilion?

Either prospect made Wend's stomach twist with worry.

Daggitt didn't return until sundown, when he banged open the cabin door and staggered toward the table. A deer, dressed for the spit, was draped over his shoulders.

He flung the deer onto the table. "Cook it."

Wend eyed the deer dripping blood onto the newly scrubbed table. "Where did you get it?"

Daggitt's grin sent chills down Wend's spine. "A *friend* over the hill."

Wend folded his arms. "I'm not eating stolen food."

"Starve, for all I care, but cook it good, or I'll take out your eye like that cat."

"I can't carry it."

"Don't push it, kid," Daggitt grumbled, but he carried the deer to the fire in the clearing.

Wend had never cooked deer, but he prepared it as best he could, trying to recall how his mother had salted and rubbed the meat with forest herbs. He found salt in one of the cabin cupboards. The sunny ground between the trees and the village was home to rosemary and garlic. He would have added berries, but they were out of season.

He kept the fire low and roasted the venison slowly. The juices sputtered in the flames, and the smoky aroma made his mouth water. All he'd eaten all day was a piece of stale flatbread. But the image of Daggitt's knife, dripping red, was enough to steel his will.

I won't eat stolen food.

Morning was a gray glimmer in the east. Wend slipped off the boat with a lantern in hand and headed to the village. When he got to the first house, he lit the lantern and began to explore. The house had been picked clean, as was the next one. In the third house, he found a length of fishing line and a short, notched stick. Two doors down, he found a jumble of tackle.

The stream was pink and gold when he returned to the clearing. He hadn't found a fishing pole, but now that the sun was up, he could make one. After cutting a four-foot branch from a willow sapling, he wrapped his line twice around the end of the pole and tied it off with two half hitches. He set out the hooks he had found. Two were made from fish bones that had been lashed together. The third was a J-shaped hook carved from deer antler. He selected one of the fish-bone hooks that had a sharp point and tied it to the end of his line with a Palomar knot. For a bobber, he tied a piece of cottonwood bark onto his line with string. He attached his sinker, a stone with a drilled hole, a foot above the hook.

He set the pole aside and collected insect larvae, worms, and a cricket from beneath rocks and logs. After returning to his pole, he slapped a worm so it would stop wriggling and attached it to the hook.

For luck, he fingered the wishbone tip Leena had given him. He took a deep breath, was about to throw his first cast, when he saw Daggitt watching him from the boat.

Wend held his pole high. "Look what the stream brought!"

"Ha! Joke's on you. A river snake will pull you under and the muddy bottom will be your grave."

"I'm strong enough now. No snake's going to get *me*."

Wend cast his line far into the stream. Daggitt watched, as if waiting for vindication that Wend would be pulled under.

Wend ignored him. His attention was on the bobber, which lay flat on the water. This late in the morning, he expected the fish had eaten and would be lazy, but after a few minutes, the bobber tipped under on one side. Wend gave his line a quick jerk. Then he began winding his line around the notched stick. A trout came out of the water. Twenty-four inches of wriggling gold.

The Stream

Wend held up the fish for Daggitt to see. "Look what the stream brought me!"

Daggitt cursed, grabbed his jug, and stalked off to the village.

Next morning, Wend and Daggitt saw the cat again. It looked thinner and skittish as it cut across a corner of the clearing. Fear tinged its eyes.

And desperation.

It slipped into the foliage without giving them a glance.

It was so friendly, thought Wend. *How could it change so fast?*

"*That's* what the stream does," said Daggitt.

Wend didn't know what to say.

The stream sent an answer the next day when a ceramic jar floated down the current right into Wend's hands. He held it up triumphantly. Daggitt scowled, flung himself into the hammock, and uncorked his jug.

The debate continued over the following months. Daggitt barged into the cabin and showed Wend a baby robin that had fallen from its nest.

"See? See?" Daggitt said.

"But you brought it to me," Wend replied. He fed the baby . . . until the bird disappeared. Wend didn't want to think about what Daggitt did with it.

A storm blew in, raging for days. The stream swelled and ran muddy. Their supply of fresh water, stored in jugs and skins, grew low.

Daggitt held up a near-empty water skin. "*This* is what we get, boy. Scraping and clawing for everything."

When the storm passed, Wend was up early looking for gifts. A sealed basket came bobbing on the current. Inside he found a sack of acorn flour, a jar he could hold bait in, and a ceramic pot with a lid. Thirty minutes later, he was slow-baking a largemouth bass, rare where the stream lacked depth, as it did here. The pot was nestled on hot coals. The aroma of laurel, garlic, and mushrooms filled the morning air and drew Daggitt from the cabin. He squatted by the fire and glowered as he stared at the oven.

When the fish was done, Wend removed the lid and offered some to Daggitt. Daggitt swore and stalked off to the village, his jug tipped high.

One day something big pulled the fishing pole from Wend's hands. He stared in dismay as it sank.

Daggitt watched with a satisfied smirk, and said mockingly, "Look what the stream brought me."

It rained bitterly for two days, preventing Wend from fashioning another rod. The first dry day, he made another pole, and a net too. Soon he was pulling out enough fish for both of them.

The Stream

"The stream brings enough for both of us. You can stop stealing and killing," he said.

"But not enough for your mates." Daggitt nodded toward the boys' camp.

"I can teach them. There'll be enough for all of us."

"The stream brings pain and suffering."

Anger and frustration welled up in Wend, and a good dose of Leena's hot temper. "You don't work, you don't fish. Or hunt, or build anything your own."

"Why work when others do it for me?"

"My father said that a man who doesn't work isn't a man at all."

Daggitt slammed his fist onto the table so hard Wend thought it would break. "I'll take whatever I want from this blasted world. Give as I've gotten."

During these months, Wend saw a pattern. When Daggitt's food grew low, he staged a raid. First he trod up the trail, Wend guessed, to select his victim. Then he paddled the canoe across the stream and went into Nick's tent. That night, he and the boys slipped like shadows over the hill.

As soon as Wend saw these signs, he tied the bandanna on the awning pole. He hadn't seen Purlo since the day they were separated. He could only hope that Purlo was somehow watching him.

Wend was never taken on the raids. He and Daggitt both knew he would warn the victim.

❖

Wildflowers and grass were drying on the hills. A sick feeling had been growing inside Wend for some time. Something terrible must have happened to Purlo. He couldn't have remained hidden for so long. At some point, Wend saw every other boy from the camp.

Wend decided to cross the stream to find out what had happened to Purlo. He would go when Daggitt went on his next raid.

The debate came to a head, first. Daggitt had been showing up at odd times to launch into his latest argument.

This time he crashed through the cabin door, drunk as a skunk, his face triumphant. "What did the stream bring you? *Me!*"

Over the next hours, Daggitt complained of pain in his head, neck, and shoulders. His cure was a belt of nummrak down the throat, and often.

"You should rest," said Wend.

"Forget it, kid. Fire juice will fix it."

By evening, he was too weak to stand. Wend helped him to bed. Daggitt shook like a leaf from chills. Wend piled on blankets.

Thirty minutes later, Daggitt threw them off. "I'm burning up." He tried to get out of bed. Wend nudged him back. Daggitt pushed him aside and stood. He flapped his arms like a huge, ungainly bird, and then toppled back into bed. "See what your damn stream brings."

Wend stayed with him, wiping his brow, chest, and arms with a damp cloth when he was hot, and covering him when he was cold. Daggitt demanded his jug, but Wend dumped the contents overboard and instead spooned into the man's mouth fish broth or tea made from boneset or elderberry.

Deep into the night, Daggitt began muttering. Most of what he said was incoherent, but Wend caught snatches when Daggitt cried out.

"I'm coming, I'm coming . . . Please, no. No!" Daggitt gripped Wend's arms until he thought they would snap.

Daggitt didn't seem to recognize him. "Water — water everywhere . . ."

Wend eased him back to the pillow. He dipped cloth into a bowl of cool stream water and mopped Daggitt's face.

"Smashed, all smashed . . ."

"It's okay," Wend said. "You're here. Safe."

"Bodies . . . a river of bodies . . . floating . . ."

Wend patted with the cloth. "You're safe now."

"Ghosts . . . ghosts of the dead . . . Water . . . water . . . water . . ."

Three days passed before the fever broke. Daggitt was too weak to leave his bed. When he could tolerate food, Wend spooned leek soup into his mouth. In a day, he was able to take in fish. He ate what Wend caught until he was well enough and strong enough to realize they had run out of stolen food. Then he sent the food Wend had prepared flying across the room.

He rose from the bed and stood on shaky legs. "It's all pain and agony, kid. Don't let anyone tell you different."

"But the stream brought you me."

Daggitt's face turned redder than at the peak of the fever. With a strangled cry he lurched from the cabin.

Wend tried to stop him, but the man shoved him aside and staggered toward the village.

Wend knew better than to follow. Daggitt was weak, but not so weak that a backhand wouldn't draw stars.

He didn't return until the following afternoon. He wove across the clearing with a jug in his hand. When he reached the boat, he took a swig and then smashed the jug on the prow. Wend was on the upper deck, mending a corner of awning that had torn loose.

"Get down here," Daggitt called.

Wend climbed down the ladder. Daggitt grabbed him by the collar and dragged him off the boat. He shoved Wend along the shore toward the spare raft.

"Get on," said Daggitt when they reached the raft.

Wend stepped aboard. He had no idea what Daggitt was planning, but he knew it wasn't good. The man's face was inflamed, his eyes dark, cold stones. Wend's heart took off like rapids.

"Give me the pole and paddle," said Daggitt.

"No . . ."

Daggitt took a threatening step. "Do it, or I'll snap your neck."

Wend held out the pole and paddle, but clutched them so that Daggitt had to pull them from his hands.

"Sit. In the middle of the raft."

Wend sank to the rough planking. The raft was empty now. No food. No water. No fishing pole. No knife. He looked around, desperately, hoping beyond hope that someone was nearby to help. That Purlo had escaped somehow and had formed a gang with Gan and his friends, and they would save him.

Daggitt followed his gaze to the boy's camp. "Joke's on you, kid. Your friend took off the first night."

"He wouldn't leave without me."

"He did. Let me tell you what the stream is. It's a vicious snake that will chew you up and spit you out. You hear me? Tear you up with its teeth."

Daggitt gave the raft a tremendous shove and launched it into the stream. Wend sent water flying as he paddled with his hands, desperately trying to get to the boys' camp. To Purlo.

The current was too swift and carried him downstream.

Daggitt called after him. "You'll see, kid. A waterfall worse than any you could imagine. It's the end of the world.

Chapter Nine

Adrift

The emptiness of the raft made it seem bigger. The stream widened, dwarfing the raft, and the treelined shores seemed to recede to an unreachable distance, until Wend felt he was only a speck. He was five again, bobbing blind down the stream in a basket.

He had always feared Daggitt would explode at any moment. Looking back, he wondered why something like this had not happened sooner. By rights, he should have been beaten or his neck snapped long ago.

Now Daggitt was behind him, and for once, he did not long to go upstream.

Little by little, the terrors melted away . . .

He had survived a storm, cataracts, and Daggitt. He was on a good, sturdy raft. He would survive this.

Only thoughts of Purlo made him ache. If Daggitt was lying, Wend's friend was in the hands of pirates. He could only hope Daggitt was telling the truth, and Purlo had escaped to his uncle.

He tried paddling with his hands but was unable to make any headway or steer to shore. If a giant cataract did mark the end of the world, there would be no way to stop from going over.

But he felt certain Daggitt did not know what lay ahead. No one did . . . except Wend had seen, from the summit of the hill overlooking the tributaries, many silver strands converging on one mighty river that disappeared into mist. Did the mist rise where all the water of the world fell unceasingly?

He had no idea, and for now, he didn't care. He was alive. He was dry. It was summer; the night was warm.

In a moment of blissful surrender, he sat and let the stream take him where it would.

Chapter Ten

Survival

Next morning, Wend woke and found that the current had carried him to a sandy shore, lined with laurels, sycamores, buckeyes, and higher up, a few pines. He splashed his face with water, and beached the raft.

His last meal had been yesterday afternoon, and a hungry animal growled inside his stomach.

To survive, he needed three things: knife, fire, and spear.

He started with the knife. He had never made one, but he'd watched his father release blades from rock, and Wend had been sent to find the best stones.

Up to his knees in the stream, he looked for a good oval hammer rock. The stream bottom was covered with stones, and it wasn't hard to find one he could wield with his right hand. He wanted large rocks to chip blades from, and he looked for triangular ones that were well weathered and had an edge on one side. After returning to the beach with the best candidates, he tested the sound of each by striking them with his hammer stone. He discarded rocks that sounded dull and kept two that produced a ringing clack.

He sat on a log on a level part of the beach, took off his shirt, folded it, and laid it across his left thigh. He placed one of the triangular rocks on the shirt, then picked up the hammer stone and took a couple of slow practice swings, to get the feeling of the arc. With a prayer to the gods, he struck the edge of the rock with his hammer, blinking on impact in case pieces flew into his eyes. When he opened his eyes, he saw a large, sharp blade at his feet.

After drawing out blade after blade, he tested them with his finger. Only then did he allow himself to smile.

Holding up one of the knives, he shouted, "See, Daggitt?! See what the stream brought?!"

He pocketed his blades and turned his attention to building a fire. Besides flint and steel, he had used a bow drill. He had no twine to make the bow, so he decided to make a fire plow. In the woods, he spotted a fallen laurel in a bed of ivy. With his knife, he cut a small branch for his plow, and fashioned a dull point. The tree had splintered. After breaking off a chunk from the jagged edge, he carved a groove down its center.

He set the stick and grooved wood aside and collected dried grass, twigs, branches, and small logs. He formed a bird's nest out of the grass, and carried the fire plow, wood, and tinder back to the beach, where he cleared a flat space and ringed it with stones from the stream. Kneeling, he put the stick's point into the groove and plowed back and forth rapidly. Wisps of smoke rose from the groove. He continued plowing until the smoke made him cough and the hot dust in the groove turned to coal.

Then, with the bird's nest cradled in one hand, he tapped the coal into the tinder, and blew on it gently. This moment, when flames burst from tinder, was far more mysterious than anything he had seen in the Pavilion.

The magic of the gods was his: He breathed fire into being.

When the fire crackled, he returned to the woods and searched for a sapling. He found a pine, no thicker than a walking staff, and cut it down at the base. With the base at his feet, he measured a length to the tips of his fingers held over his head, and then cut the remaining portion at the top. He laid the top of the spear on a log. After bisecting the circumference, he carefully sliced eight inches down the pole. Then he pushed a stick the width of his pinky to the bottom of the slice, spreading the ends of the pole into two prongs. His blade had become dull, so he discarded it and selected another. In a few minutes, he had carved sharp points on the two ends.

When he returned to the fire, it was red-hot and licking from the bottom of the logs. He held the spear tips over the flames, turning and turning them until, testing them with his finger, he judged them fire-hardened. Then he rose and strode over to the stream, where three large rocks with flat tops stepped into the water. He leaped from rock to rock until he was perched on the last with his spear.

Smaller rocks nearby diverted the current, leaving water calm and clear down to the silt bottom.

Wend waited.

The sun beat down.

Sweat trickled down his face.

After an hour, he retreated to the second rock and waited. Still no fish. Returning to the third rock, he sat and watched the water. A mosquito hovered near his ear. He waved it away.

By early afternoon, he had still not speared a fish. The sun blistered. He knelt and drank from the stream, then skipped back to the second rock.

At last, he saw a trout swim toward him, but at the last moment, it darted away into a forest of hydrilla.

The current flowed with the lazy pace of summer. Wend plunged chest-high into the stream and waded to the opposite shore, where a semicircle of rocks stepped into the water and offered nooks for fish to lurk.

He knelt on the last stone and studied the shadowy edges where rock sank into silt. A trout hovered near the bottom.

Wend rose, poised his spear, aimed, and thrust. The water made the fish appear nearer than it was. Wend missed. The fish darted away.

He moved to another rock, where the streambed dipped deeper. Lurking near the bottom beside his rock was eighteen inches of silver. Wend dipped his spear slowly into the water and noted the way the end bent. He adjusted his aim and then struck, pinning the fish.

Back at the fire, he sharpened a stick and roasted the trout on one end, turning it over the flames.

He ate the fish off the stick. When he was done, he left an offering for the stream.

The current slowed. The water sank, gradually; but the heat and the fish stayed, and so did Wend. He thought little about Daggitt, Nick, or even Purlo. Every waking thought was on survival.

His senses sharpened, attuned to the sound of the stream, the calls of the birds, the motion of the trees.

He caught the scents of deer and wild boar. Boar were dangerous, but also a potential source of food. He heard them in the distance, stampeding through the underbrush.

In the early days, he built a lean-to, laying poles against the fat end of a log and then covering the poles with laurel branches thick with leaves. He crawled inside for shade during the day, and when the nights were warm, he slept beside the embers of his fire.

Under starlight, his hands were busy. He made a spoon and bowl, burning out the insides with hot coals. He carved a pole and paddle for his raft. The moon saw him twisting bark fibers and braiding them into fishing line, rope, and a basket. On days when he caught more than one fish, he smoked what he couldn't eat in maple leaves.

One night, when summer had eased into the hotter days of fall, Wend trapped a boar. To celebrate, he stripped off his clothes and painted his face with red clay.

He danced and whooped around the roasting pig. "I make fire. I fish. I have a pole, paddle, knife, and spear. See, Daggitt?" he sang. "See?"

That night he dreamed that Daggitt's bear-hands reached for him. He awoke in a sweat, *I'll snap their necks* ringing in his ears.

If you call the devil, he'll come, Wend thought, and vowed not to speak the name again.

Brown, gold, and carmine floated downstream. Wend launched his raft, drifting with the leaves. The scent of rain was in the air.

It was not a lack of fish, shelter, fire, or the threat of storm that lashed him on. It was loneliness.

And the vague memory of blue-black hair and eyes like stars . . .

Chapter Eleven

A Strange Man

Wend had seen no one on the stream for days. The sun set, leaving the land in twilight. The air was cold. Clouds piled on the horizon. The trees shunned both shores. Beyond, hills rolled away, lonely and desolate.

He was surprised to see smoke curling up beyond a bend in the stream. He snatched up his pole and hurried downstream with all the strength he could muster.

Rounding the bend, he saw a few straggly trees and a cabin nestled beside a dead oak. Nearby was a meager garden, a chopping block, and a woodpile. Much of the ground between cabin and stream was covered with baskets, as tall as a man. A boat, beached high on the bank, was almost buried under a jumble of blackberry vines and grass scorched flaxen by the sun.

He saw no dock or pole to tie his raft to, so Wend pulled it from the stream and left it near the boat. A weaving course through the baskets took him to the cabin door, where he knocked. When no one answered, he tried again. The only sound came from a flock of geese flying overhead.

He was about to walk around back when a tall man rounded the corner of the cabin. His hair was long and matted. A beard, falling to his chest, was black and shot with gray. Soiled and torn clothes hung loose on his frame, as if he had once worn several sizes larger.

He wheeled an empty barrow, his gaze fixed on the ground.

"Hello," said Wend.

The man's body jerked so hard the wheel of the barrow rattled.

"I'm sorry," said Wend, "I didn't mean to startle you."

The man set down the barrow and looked in disbelief toward the desolate hills. "No one crosses that . . ."

"I came from the stream."

"The where . . ." The man looked everywhere but the water singing softly not many feet away.

"The stream?"

The man began wheeling the barrow, threading through the baskets toward a stand of leafless oaks, whose branches, twisting blindly, lined the edge of the clearing.

Wend followed. "What are the baskets for?"

"Rain."

"Why?"

At the perimeter of the clearing, the man stopped before a deep, circular hole. "To drink."

Wend looked over his shoulder toward the stream. Enough water for a village flowed and bubbled between its banks.

The man picked up a shovel and then eased into the hole. The top came to his chest. He began digging, depositing each load of earth in a pile not far from Wend's feet.

"What are you digging?" Wend asked.

"A well."

"Why don't you get water from the stream?"

The man plunged the shovel into the earth, where it shuddered a moment. He mopped his brow with a tattered sleeve, then ran his fingers up and down the handle. His pinky caught a splinter, which he extracted with his teeth. Taking up the shovel, he began digging. "Never heard of it."

In a flash, Wend understood, remembering the shaggy man he and the old monk had seen chopping wood near the riverbank. The old monk's words came back to him: *He's forgotten that it's there. Such a man is far from the Ocean.*

"Your baskets will fill," said Wend. "I smell rain coming."

"I smell nothing." The man climbed out of the hole and dusted a cloud of dirt off his clothes. "Except rotting wood."

Wend could smell that too, beneath the aroma of the stream, earth, and baskets. In the dimming light, he saw the motion of a branch deeper in the trees and knew that a squirrel lingered there.

"What do you eat?" he asked.

"Eggs. Birds."

A few cold stars twinkled above, and Wend rubbed his arms. "Can I stay the night?" He hoped he could stay longer. Even this strange man would be company, and he didn't want to be on the stream when winter came.

"I have only for myself."

"I won't be any trouble."

They walked toward the cabin, winding through the maze of baskets.

"I'll catch us breakfast," Wend said hopefully. "You don't need to feed me."

They paused at the door. The man gazed at Wend, exploring him from top to bottom as if he were a strange, mythical creature. "Where in the world did you come from?" he said, with a shake of his head.

The man led Wend into a simple, one-room cabin. Built in one corner was a stone fireplace, where pots, plates, and other cooking utensils were arranged neatly beside a stool. To one side of the stool was a straw mat and folded bed furs. The rest of the room was barren, save for a table and chair. A window on the eastern wall was the only source of sunlight. A few bulbs of garlic and onion hung from the ceiling.

The man stirred the coals and fanned up flames. He lit a twig and, carrying it to the table, lit a candle. Returning to the fire, he began dressing a duck.

Wend sat cross-legged nearby and watched him work. "Did you trap him?"

"Bow and arrow."

"Where?"

The man pointed upward.

"You shot him out of the air?! You must be good," said Wend.

The man worked silently.

"Does anyone live with you?" Wend asked.

"No one."

"Did they ever?"

The man stared into the fire, his face a statue. At last, he began working again, pulling out the breast, liver, and heart. When the duck was dressed, he handed Wend a pot. "Go get water."

Wend ran outside with the pot. He could easily have filled the pot from the stream, but he was curious about the baskets. He found a smaller one that was empty and inspected it. The weave was neat and tight.

On the outside, a thin layer of sun-hardened clay made it watertight.

Using the empty basket as a stool, Wend looked inside a dozen of the taller baskets. Each was almost empty. At last, he found one that was a quarter full.

He filled the pot and returned to the man, who then stewed the duck with a few tired vegetables.

The man brought the stool to the table, where they ate silently. He had cut off the skin, thick with fat, to toast later in the fire. Besides the breast, little meat remained on the duck.

Wend had already eaten, and he only picked at his plate so the man would have more.

After dinner, the man toasted the pieces of skin and put them aside for breakfast.

"The well won't dig itself," he said, unfolding his bed furs, "I'll be up early."

Wend curled up near the fire with a deerskin that he'd found in a deserted village. When the man was snoring, Wend crept outside and filled as many of the baskets with stream water as he could before sleep tugged him back inside.

Before gray tinged the eastern horizon, Wend pulled a trout from the water. No smoke curled from the chimney, so he left the fish in a basket and explored the man's boat. He found steel and flint in the cabin and lit a candle.

The Stream

Wend had never seen a finer cabin. A table was attached to the stern wall. No storm would tip the storage baskets, held in place with horizontal slats top and bottom. Two built-in beds had pull-out drawers beneath them. Arranged in a circle near one of the bed pillows were a toy boat, fishing pole, and three tiny fish carved from wood. Wend blew dust off one of the fish and put it in his pocket.

The man squatted by a crackling fire when Wend returned with his catch. Wend cooked the fish with onions and some of the duck skin and set it on the table.

The man sniffed the food suspiciously.

"Try it," said Wend.

The man tasted the food. His brow crinkled a moment, and then his head rolled back, his mouth parted, and he gazed off.

"Do you remember?"

The man grunted in reply, but he didn't stop eating until he had sucked the bones clean. When he was done, he held the spine up and studied it. "What is it?"

Wend reached into his pocket and held out the toy fish.

The man stared at the toy. Light, seemingly from the fireplace, smoldered in his eyes and then died. He rose, took the toy from Wend's hand, walked to the fire, and tossed it into the flames. Then he stalked to the door. With his back to Wend, he said, "Leave. Don't come back."

Chapter Twelve

The Boatbuilder

Wend headed up the path toward the village, the first he'd seen on the stream in days, hugging the deerskin around his shoulders to fend off the morning chill. A small boy approached, two water jugs suspended from the ends of a pole balanced over his shoulders.

"Hello," Wend called. "Let me help you."

The boy stared as he passed and continued down to the stream.

Wend stopped at the first hut. Stakes fenced a dirt yard, where a woman sat on a stool and milked a goat.

Wend called, "I can milk her for you."

The woman stopped milking and looked Wend up and down. "There's nothing for you here. Move along."

He crossed the street. In the yard of the next house, a woman stirred clothes in a steaming pot suspended over a fire. Two girls and a boy wrestled in the dust nearby.

"I can cut wood for your fire," Wend said to the woman.

"We've got wood," she replied.

"I'll catch you breakfast."

"Get on. We don't need another waif."

Wend moved up and down the streets, offering to mend fishing nets, weave baskets, and repair a door flopping on its hinges. One woman, cracking acorns with a stone, summed up the village attitude: "We can't take every orphan that washes ashore. We've got enough mouths to feed."

Wend continued downstream. The nights brought stinging cold, but colder were the stares that greeted him at the next village. One woman let him sleep under her porch, and then turned him out the next morning. Nodding toward the five dirty-faced children who stared at Wend from the window, she said, "I've taken my share."

At the next village, three men working a fishing weir stopped him from coming ashore. He slept that night shivering in a ditch, despite having covered the top with branches and a mountain of leaves.

In the next hamlet, children were whisked inside and doors slammed before Wend could offer to work for his keep. At last, he reached a hut at the edge of the village, apart from the other buildings and closer to the stream. Two cottonwoods framed the house. Against flood, stones at the corners raised the dwelling a foot and a half off the ground. Four steps led to a porch and the front door, which was open. Smoke rose from a stone chimney.

To the left of the house was a woodshed. Closer to shore, a man stood beside a half-built boat, studying it. Wend approached to get a better look at the man and the boat. The morning sun had not yet melted a thin sheet of ice on the ground.

As Wend drew near, his foot crunched the ice. The man turned at the sound, gazed at Wend a moment, and turned back to the boat. A curl of smoke rose from a pipe balanced between his lips. Except for a few wisdom lines, the skin on his face was soft as a baby's. His eyes were the color of trees reflected in water.

"That's going to be a beautiful boat," said Wend.

"All boats are beautiful," the man replied. "They float."

Wend thought of Daggitt's boat. "I saw one that wasn't. It was a patchwork of a dozen boats."

"Broken pieces have their beauty."

The man put on an apron covered with sawdust and reached for a long two-by-four. Though the man's hands were large and powerful—with thick fingers and knuckles like stones—Wend grasped the other end of the lumber and helped him carry it to a sawhorse.

Wend held the wood in place while the man measured and sawed it in a few easy strokes.

The man looked at Wend, a whisper of a smile creasing his lips, as if he'd taken satisfaction in what he had just done.

"You're good," said Wend.

"The saw does the work."

The man carried the lumber through the ribs of the hull and laid it lengthwise along the keel. Like the saw, his hammer knew its job, nailing the wood with a few effortless blows.

He spoke little, his work unhurried. Wend sensed that chatter would be as welcome as a squawking crow. He hovered nearby. When he noticed the man running low on nails, Wend fetched more from a bucket. When the plans for the boat lifted and fluttered in the breeze, he held them down. When one sheet blew across the ground, he found a piece of coal so the man could redraw it. Then Wend anchored the drawing with stones on the corners.

The day passed like the stream in summer. The man didn't pause to eat, and Wend felt no hunger. His mind was consumed with one idea: to be a boatbuilder.

The sun was tucking below the horizon when the man said, "How did you get here?"

"My raft."

"The villagers snatch anything unguarded. If they don't get it, the stream might."

All the way back to the raft, Wend puzzled over the man's words. Were they his way of saying, Thanks for the help, kid; now shove off? The raft was where he'd left it, a little upstream. He climbed aboard, blew into his hands, and rubbed them before taking up the pole and setting off. He felt weary in his bones, not from working, but from days of living close to fireplaces and homes, and never being part of the warmth inside. Hunger leaped into his gut and growled like a starving cat.

He neared the man's hut. Smoke and the aroma of bacon rose from the chimney. The man sat on a bench on the porch. His pipe glowed in the dimming light.

Wend waved. In the twilight, he couldn't be certain if the man nodded, or if the raising and lowering of his pipe was a slight wave. Wend beached the raft. As he approached the hut, the man stood, turned, and walked through the door.

When Wend reached the door, it was still open. He hovered there. The man hadn't lit a candle. From the darkness, he heard him say, "What are you waiting for?"

Wend entered. "What's your name?"

"Dory."

Wend intended to be up before the sun to catch breakfast. But the cold air in the hut kept him buried in his bed furs. He half woke, then slipped back into a dream.

The aroma of sizzling bacon roused him, followed by a belligerent cock-a-doodle-doo.

Dory squatted, turning bacon on a griddle. "This would go well with eggs. If someone could get past that rooster."

Wend crawled out of the cocoon of blankets and stretched. "I'll get them."

He grabbed a basket from a shelf and was out back in a blink. The chicken hut was rank with droppings, which pebbled and crusted the floor and nests like hardened lava. The chickens scratched in the dirt floor, looking for insects and worms, but the rooster, which had a bright orange cape, stood guard beside one of the nests. He glanced at Wend indifferently and crowed. It seemed to Wend that he didn't crow for the sun or his mates, but for the pleasure of hearing his own voice.

Wend gathered half a dozen eggs and returned to Dory's hut.

Dory glanced up from the bacon. "That rooster give you any problems?"

"Naw."

Dory's brow arched in surprise. He lifted Wend's arms by the wrists and looked them up and down.

"Humph," he said, and turned back to the bacon with a frown.

After breakfast, Wend started to collect the dishes.

"What are you doing?" Dory packed his pipe and lit it, sending up puffs of aromatic smoke.

"I was going to wash them."

"You're not my servant."

"I got the eggs."

"I didn't ask you for them."

Wend shifted uncertainly on his feet. He studied Dory's face but couldn't read it. Perhaps he was just giving Wend a good breakfast before sending him downstream.

Dory nodded to one of the walls, where a guitar and flutes of various sizes hung. "Do you play?"

"I played drums with the monks. I could play on your table."

"You're not here to entertain me."

Dory finished his pipe. They fetched two buckets of stream water. On the porch, they washed and dried their plates and utensils. Afterward, Dory stood gazing at the boat while the sun rose. Wend stood beside him, wondering if he was outliving his welcome.

Dory put on his apron. "A man needs a boat."

"That's what my father said."

Nodding toward the raft, Dory asked, "Did you build that?"

"No."

"You better learn how. A man needs to float."

Wend pointed at the pile of logs Dory cut lumber from. "I could build a raft from some of that."

"Well, that's what you better do." Dory picked up a long four-by-four and began sawing.

"By myself?"

Dory led Wend down to the stream. Picking up a thumb-size piece of driftwood, he submerged it underwater and let it go. The wood sprang to the surface.

He laid his hand on Wend's shoulder. "No matter what the stream does, you've got to float. Do you understand?"

"Yes, sir."

Dory returned to his sawhorse, giving Wend no further mind.

Balancing a twig from his lips, as if it were a pipe, Wend studied Daggitt's raft, and decided he'd make something smaller and lighter. He'd watched men building rafts. They worked as a team, rolling logs into shallow water. With a man on each side, they could hold the logs in place. But Wend couldn't lash the logs by himself. They would float away.

He needed a different plan.

He rolled six logs off the top of the pile and laid them side by side. Then he selected three about a foot wide and discarded the others. He rolled more logs from the pile, judging them for size, until he had six that matched.

In the woodshed he found a saw, hammer, and chisel. After returning with the tools, he measured the logs, propped one atop another, and began sawing.

Dory had been working inside the hull of his boat, but now he was behind Wend, his hand on Wend's saw hand, guiding it.

"Relax. Let it glide."

As soon as Wend got the feel of the saw, Dory was back at his boat, hammering.

Wend rolled the cut logs near the shore, where he arranged them in a rectangle. He returned to the woodpile, where he found two logs that were six inches wide. These he measured, cut, and rolled to the rectangle.

He chewed on his twig, considering how to lash the pieces together. He was unaware that Dory had stopped hammering until he saw the man standing close by, cupping his chin in his hand, studying Wend's work.

Dory squatted, picked up a stick, and drew in the dirt. "You could cut a dovetail notch."

"A foot and a half from each end?" asked Wend.

"That'd be about right."

Wend marked off where the grooves would go, and cut two inches deep with his saw. With hammer and chisel, he began paring away wood.

The sun's afterglow glimmered on the water. Only half

the notches were cut, but Wend and Dory put away their tools, stripped, and plunged into the cold stream, where they washed away dirt, sweat, and sawdust. Then they dashed to the hut, wrapped themselves in blankets, and sat by the fire.

"Dory?"

"Yes."

"How long will I be staying?"

Dory took his pipe from his mouth and sent a smoke ring to the ceiling. "A man isn't a man until he's built his own boat."

On the third day, Wend lashed his crossbeams into place and was ready to test his raft.

"It's too heavy for you to drag to the water," said Dory.

Wend pointed to clouds piling on the horizon. "When it rains, the stream will come to me."

Dory grinned and clapped him on the back. Together they drove a stake into the ground and tied the raft with a stout rope. The rain passed in the night. Next morning, half of the raft floated in the water. Wend threw on his pole and pushed the raft into the stream. He and Dory leaped aboard. Wend untied the rope, took up his pole, and steered into the current.

"I can float!" he cried. "I can float!"

"Easy." Dory laughed. "Or we'll end up downstream."

They beached the raft on the opposite shore and sat eating apples that hung from the trees.

"Dory?"

"Hmm?"

"You didn't say how long I'd be staying."

"Well, now, you've built a raft. But before you build a boat, you need to make a canoe. That's good work for the cold months."

"I reckon it'll take all winter."

"I reckon it will."

Wend started on the canoe as soon as they were back. He found a fallen cottonwood behind the chicken coop. He wished it was closer to Dory's boat so the man could keep an eye on him, but the tree would be impossible for the two of them to move.

With coal, Wend sketched several views of the canoe on a piece of bark, and showed his ideas to Dory.

"You're good." Dory grinned. "A little steeper angle on the prow, and you've got it."

Wend spent the morning stripping bark from the cottonwood with an adze. Next, he drew the first cutting lines, then began sawing where one end of the canoe would be. It was hard, slow work. He neared the bottom by evening and stopped for the day. Next morning, he dug a hole beneath the tree so his saw would cut clean through. By evening, both ends of the canoe were cut.

But a problem gnawed at him. He discussed it with Dory over dinner.

"I need to roll my canoe away from the tree," said Wend.

"I've been thinking about that too," Dory replied.

"A lever won't do it, even with the two of us."

Dory swirled cider around his cup and gazed at the foam. "We need help."

"The villagers wouldn't let me sleep under their porch. They won't lift a finger."

"You need to give them something."

"Like what?"

"How about that damn rooster?"

Wend laughed. "They're not going to do it for a rooster."

"No, I suppose not." Dory speared a piece of trout and ate it thoughtfully. "Rafts are valuable around here. You've got two."

"I could give up Daggitt's raft. But how will that help? I can only give it to one person. It'll take twenty people to move that tree."

Dory grinned. "Raffle it. We need some excitement around here."

Wend was doubtful about Dory's plan, but next morning he went door to door. Most of the villagers had seen his raft the day he arrived. Those who hadn't stopped by Dory's place for a look. It was a strong, sturdy raft. An extra one would come in handy or could be traded. Soon, children followed Wend around as he handed out pieces of bark with numbers on them. They wanted that raft too, and Wend gave numbers to children older than five.

A dozen men carried the raft to a central square in the village. Then the whole village followed Wend back to the cottonwood. They crowded around the twelve-foot length Wend had cut for his canoe. Men leaned against the top, women at the middle, and the children wriggled between their legs to get their hands on the bottom.

The first try, the tree rolled a few inches and settled back.

"It's too heavy," a red-faced woman said. "What do I need a raft for, anyway?"

"Give me your number, Lizbeth," a man called.

"I wouldn't give you my number if you were the last man on the stream," replied Lizbeth.

"Then give it to me," said another woman. "I'm going to trade that raft for a sack of flour."

"Over my dead body," said Lizbeth. She returned to the tree and everyone tried to roll it again, without success.

Dory shooed the crowd aside, lit his pipe, and studied the tree. "Tie some ropes around it. We can pull from one side and work levers on the other."

Half a dozen boys ran for shovels, spades, and ropes. The excavation went quickly with people working both sides of the tree. Four ropes were pushed beneath the tree with a stick and then tied around the trunk. Men lined up on one side of the tree with levers and fulcrums. Women and children piled onto the ropes like it was a tug-of-war, humans against the cottonwood. Wend was certain that old tree would win, but with a heave they rolled it clear.

Everyone wanted to celebrate. Several women started a fire and roasted duck. People brought mead, cheese, flatbread, turban soup in the gourd, walnut dumplings, and maple syrup. After they ate, they gathered around Wend. He reached into a basket and stirred the pieces of bark. Drawing one piece, he called out, "Fifteen. Who's got fifteen?"

The raft went to a mother with two small children. Wend followed everyone back to the central square. He watched as a dozen men carried the raft around a corner and away to her house. That was the first night he didn't dream about people upstream.

Wend worked several weeks squaring the log and shaping the prow. He felt no desire to play with the village children. After the raffle, they were as indifferent to him as when he had arrived. Wend didn't mind. He felt hungry for Dory, as if the man could fill the years Wend had missed with his father.

It became too cold to bathe in the stream. Each evening after working, Dory had a vat of boiling water and a pair of tubs waiting near the porch. On clear nights, they settled in the steaming water, watched the stars, and talked. Wend had a million questions about boatbuilding, how to sharpen tools, how to mix pitch from pine sap. These melted away in the tub, for other questions rose with the stars.

One moonlit night, Wend asked, "Why are we on the stream?"

"Fish live in the water. We live on the stream."

"Why can't we leave it?"

"We can, but it would be a great sin."

"Why?"

Dory's fingers swept the arc of the panorama. "All of this disappears."

"Would we disappear with it?"

"Some say we would."

"What do you say?"

"I only know what's here."

When rain threatened, they covered their boats and retreated indoors, where they built shelves or laid molding by day. Night was reserved for song and dance, and Dory taught Wend how to play the flute.

Serious questions stayed outside with the tubs. Inside, Wend slipped into Leena's teasing spirit. "You're afraid of that rooster," he said one morning as he watched Dory knead dough.

Dory slapped on flour and punched the dough. "I *am* not."

"Then why don't you get the eggs?"

"That rooster's a menace."

"He never bothers me."

"Fine." Dory tossed his apron aside and stalked outside. A few minutes later he returned with eggs and a dozen red marks on his arms. "Told you he had it in for me. I hope you're satisfied."

"Why doesn't he like you?"

"Some animals are born ornery."

When the bottom of the canoe was shaped, smoothed, fire-hardened, and sealed with pitch, Wend needed to turn it. He would need the villagers again.

"What can I give now?" he asked.

"You'll have a fine canoe," Dory replied. "Raffle the other raft."

Wend fell silent. He and Dory used the raft to cross the stream, where they gathered apples, sat on the rocks, and dangled their feet over the water.

"Wend, do you remember that day I pushed the wood underwater and it sprang to the surface?"

Wend nodded.

"You're floating now. You made something of value."

Wend understood. From his hands he had created something that got him more things. He was making his way in the world. He had risen.

The raft was raffled. At the first snow, Wend began burning out the canoe. Frozen mornings surrendered to heat from the fire and hot coals. Dory hung around the canoe, saying it was too cold to work on his boat, but Wend was certain Dory wanted to oversee the burning and scraping. If the fire was too hot or burned too long, it would run down every little flaw and fissure of the wood. The whole project would be ruined.

They came home covered with soot and plunged into the tubs. Too exhausted to talk, they contemplated the constellations wheeling above and listened to a horned owl in the cottonwood.

On warmer days, Dory sometimes stopped their work and took them to the water, where they watched the ripples or studied the reflection of the trees.

"Why aren't we working on the canoe?" Wend asked.

Dory skipped a stone across the water. "So we don't get too far from the stream."

Winter waned. As work on the canoe drew to completion, Wend began to worry whether his time with Dory was ending.

On one of their breaks to the stream Wend said, "The canoe is almost done."

"It's a beauty, Wend. I never saw a finer one."

The Stream

Wend watched a butterfly dancing over the surface of the water. "What happens when it's done?"

Dory tapped ashes from his pipe and studied the bowl. "A man who can make a canoe can build a boat."

"I reckon that would take years."

"I reckon it would."

Wend helped Dory with his boat for the next two summers. He learned about hardwood and softwood, oak for the keel and frame and tough, waterproof larch for planking. He learned how to make oakum from old rope and pine pitch, and how to caulk the seams of the hull.

Dory didn't seem to be in a rush to finish, and that suited Wend. One evening under the stars, he felt a terrible longing to never leave this spot. He knew every curve of the tree line, the music of the current in winter and summer. And where the constellations would reflect in the water as they rose in the sky.

"Why can't we settle in one spot?" Wend asked, skimming his fingers along the surface of his bathwater.

Dory lathered with soap and studied the foam on his arms. "Life's as fragile as these bubbles."

"We're fixing the house like we're going to stay."

"Might as well be comfortable." Dory grinned.

"Are you gonna raffle it?

"I just might do that, if I can throw in the rooster."

"It looks like you're planning to stay awhile."

"Something lifts and carries us away." Dory climbed dripping from his tub. He grabbed a kettle off the fire and poured more hot water into their tubs. Then he settled back into the steaming water. "There are a couple of boats to build first."

Wend wasn't sure when he stopped worrying about how long he would stay. Maybe it was when Dory finished his boat and they began working on Wend's.

He could see the boat in his mind. The prow would slice through the water, and the cabin would have built-in beds, tables, and drawers. No storm would send chairs and pots flying!

Wend drew out his plans and showed them to Dory.

"Why are you bothering with built-ins?" Dory asked.

"A man has to keep his family safe."

Days were for laying down the keel and bending the hull's ribs. Nights were for singing. Dory taught Wend the upper harmonies of songs that would make the rooster blush.

One summer, three village girls started spying on Wend from behind shrubbery thirty paces from his boat.

"Why are they hanging around?" he asked Dory.

"If you don't like it, don't saw with your shirt off."

"Get rid of them."

"I don't think I can."

By the next summer, the girls brought Wend lunch baskets with honeyed duck, cold cider, and blackberry pie.

"I better get rid of them," Dory said. "You're working slower than a slug."

"Don't you dare." Wend laughed.

"They're as scrawny as she-goats."

"I know, but they can cook."

Four-by-fours that Dory carried in his big hands Wend now carried too. When the planking on the deck went down, Wend began singing the lower harmonies.

Dory shook his head. "You're as tall and wide as that cottonwood."

When the boat was near completion, Wend's saw started skipping, and his hammer hit his thumb more than the nail.

"What's got into me?" he asked Dory.

"You've got the itch."

"What's that?"

"I've been watching. You spend as much time staring at that bend in the stream as you do working."

"What do I do?

Dory mopped his brow. "Take the afternoon off. It's too hot to work, anyway."

They took the canoe across the stream, and swam to a tree trunk lodged in the water. They climbed onto the tree and sunned there until the heat drove them back into the water.

Wend gazed downstream. "I reckon a man ought to have a wife."

"I reckon he should," Dory replied.

"None of these village girls will do."

"No. They'd be as bad as that rooster."

"What will you do?"

"I reckon a man needs another man to stand at his wedding."

Tears welled in Wend's throat. "I reckon he does. What about you? I could stand at yours."

"I'm too old. Besides . . ." Dory put his arm around Wend's shoulders. "I've got a family."

In the fall of Wend's sixteenth year, he and Dory raffled the cabin, loaded their boats, and sailed together downstream.

Chapter Thirteen

Courting

The market buzzed like a hive. Men and women milled through the crowd hawking pears, peaches, and grapes. Heaping bins of carrots, squash, beans, peppers, and onions—arranged beneath awnings and umbrellas—overflowed the village square.

Wend filled his basket quickly and hurried to a small stage where he had seen a girl dancing when he'd entered the market. The knot of men in front of the stage was too tight to break through, but Wend found a spot on one side.

To the flourish of a violin, the girl danced onto the stage, the folds of her skirt spreading like wings. The music stopped when she reached center stage, and she melted to the floor. The violin, accompanied by guitar, began a slow song filled with longing. The girl rose to her knees, swept her hair aside, and swayed like an exotic underwater plant. She stood and danced in a slow circle. The tempo quickened, little by little, and the men clapped with each beat. She dipped and snapped her fingers, grabbed a fold of her dress, and held it high. Her arms undulated. She twirled. Her skirt became a swirling arabesque, more beautiful than a flower.

She closed her eyes and hugged herself. The way they stared, Wend was certain that every man in the audience imagined he was the one she embraced— Wend included.

The violin held one high note. The guitar raced on. She spun, faster and faster, hair flying like her skirt. She leaped. The music stopped as her feet touched down. Her eyes flared open and locked on Wend. As she ran from the stage, she plucked a rose from her hair and threw it to him.

Breathless, flushed from more than the day's heat, Wend wandered through the crowd in search of something to drink. He found a stand where a man whipped cold, honeyed milk to froth.

Wend joined the line of waiting customers. A voice spoke from behind. "Hello, boy in orange robes."

Wend turned. Eyes as bright as gems, surrounded by a halo of blue-black hair, gazed up at him. "Leena!" he exclaimed.

"When did you get so big?"

Wend laughed. "Dory says the chickens can't lay eggs fast enough to feed me."

She looked him up and down with a satisfied smile and nodded to his basket. "Did she weave that?"

"No, he leaves basket-making to me."

She exhaled softly and her smiled broadened. "Bad for both of you."

"I could never get the weave like yours." He pointed to his wrist, where he wore the bracelet she had given him. He had added twine to the ends to accommodate his growth.

She touched the bracelet, her thumb brushing his skin. "You kept it . . ."

"And this too." He drew the center of the wishbone from his pocket. "It never leaves me."

"Who is the rose for?"

"No one . . ."

"There isn't a Mrs. Wend?"

"No."

"A Mrs. Wend-to-be?"

"Yes." He put the rose in her hair. "It's always been you."

"You're a bold lad." She laughed, and sun on the stream never sparkled as her eyes did now.

He bought them frothy milks. She hooked her arm around his and led him through the crowd. Just outside the market, they sat on a green hillside and sipped their drinks.

She traced her finger across his upper lip. "You have a white mustache, Mr. Wend."

The afternoon passed like a dream, the dancing girl gone from his mind like a puff of smoke. As the sun set, he asked Leena to his boat for dinner.

He rushed to his boat and swabbed the deck. The deck already shone, but it gave him a channel for the currents coursing inside, as if all the rivers of the world surged within him. He tidied the cabin. Then plunged into the stream and bathed.

Dory watched from his boat, anchored nearby. "What's got into you?" he called.

"Dress up, Dory. I found Leena!"

After dinner, Leena said, "Let's see what you have in all these drawers." She began opening and scrutinizing the contents of his built-in cabinets. "Ha!"

"What's wrong?" Wend asked.

"Nothing . . . for a bachelor."

Dory took Wend aside. "Don't let this one get away."

Wend watched Leena reorganize his pots and pans. "Don't worry. I won't let her disappear again."

Before leaving, she touched Dory's arm. "Thank you for taking care of Wend."

Wend didn't need to work. To buy raffle tickets for the cabin, the villagers had loaded Wend's and Dory's boats with six months of supplies. But Wend's future was before him. If Leena wanted a ring or a necklace, he would buy it. He fished in the morning, sold his catch at the market, and squirreled away coins in a wooden box.

Leena had other ideas. Half the mornings, she whisked him away. They took long walks in the forest, and gathered wildflowers and mushrooms. They picnicked beneath a large, spreading almond tree, where she took his head in her lap, and dropped melon dripping with juice into his mouth. Once, she arrived at sunup. Grabbing his arm, she rushed him off to stamp grapes. They jumped into the vats. She lifted her skirt to her knees, and her laughter rang to the treetops.

They talked as if they had never been apart. About little nothings. About their hopes and dreams. At times, she teased him for not listening, for he only heard her voice, as if it were the song of a rare bird.

"I'm floating," he told her one evening, after escorting her home.

She took his hand between hers and lifted it. Her fingers brushed the bracelet. "May I?"

He nodded, and she removed it.

"It feels strange not having it there," he said. "I don't know if I can part with it."

"Just for a day."

He looked for her all the next day. He tried to fish, but made a mess of his tackle.

"Did I say something wrong?" he asked Dory.

"A flood couldn't tear that girl from you." Dory blew a puff of smoke and watched it curl away. "Better untangle that tackle."

Leena showed up early the next morning with a basket, half her size, made from stout cordage grass. Beaming, she set it down on Wend's deck. "Open it."

Inside, Wend found more baskets. He removed the lids, and the aroma of roast goose, wild rice, and marjoram wafted out.

She sat, tugging him down with her, and they picnicked on the deck.

"Don't eat all of it," she said. He started to ask why, but she put her finger to his lips, and said, "You'll see."

When they were done eating, she put his bracelet back on his wrist. She had extended the ends so that it fit.

"Get me two of your baskets," she said.

Wend ducked into his cabin and returned with two of his best attempts. Leena put the remaining food into them and secured the lids. Signaling him to follow, she carried the baskets down to the stream and launched them.

"Someone will need it," she said, watching them float away.

Tears sprang to Wend's eyes. Leena understood life on the stream. Her beauty, already dazzling, multiplied a thousandfold.

"Leena . . ."

She turned and gazed up at him. Now that the moment had arrived, all of the pretty lines he had rehearsed with Dory fled him.

"Yes, Mr. Wend?"

Her eyes danced. Wend could swim in them forever, but he had to get this out. "Marry me . . ."

She kissed him gently above the bracelet. "Better leave basket making to me."

The next morning, Wend dressed in his finest clothes. He ran a few drops of oil through his hair, and for once, it didn't flop every which way.

"How do I look?" he asked Dory.

Dory patted down a few wrinkles on Wend's jacket. "Like the catch of the stream."

With a shove, Wend was sent up the path to Leena's boat, his heart thumping. Her last words the night before had been, "Now all we have to do is get past my mother."

From the pink trim to the new coat of sky-blue paint, Leena's houseboat looked the same as it had the first day Wend saw it. The only addition was a cascade of wisteria that tumbled from the upper deck and down one side.

He found Leena's father, Skip, nailing a flower box below one window.

Skip looked up and grinned when he saw Wend. "Courtin', are you?"

"Yes, sir."

"A coat of paint—"

"And a few nails." Wend laughed. "I remember."

"Yep, that's how you win 'em. That's some boat you've got."

"Thank you, sir."

"What do you call her?"

"*Wend's Dream.*"

"Well, you had my permission the moment I laid eyes on you."

"Thank you, sir." Wend held another flower box in place while Skip drove in the nails. "How did you get your boat over the cataracts?"

Like the houseboat, Skip looked much the same. Mischievous eyes twinkled below the same woolen cap, only now the cap was spattered with paint. "Took her apart and lowered her, piece by piece." He nodded toward the lower deck, where Ketty sat beneath a yellow umbrella, throwing a pot. "Don't let her scare you. Her bark's worse than her bite."

Wend's heart galloped. He wished Leena was with him, but he took a deep breath and stepped onto the lower deck.

Ketty glanced at Wend's clothes and turned her attention back to the pot, which glistened in the sun. "Be a dear and turn the umbrella," she said. "No use drying up like a prune. I've told and told Leena that, but she never listens."

"She'll be beautiful forever."

"*She's* the catch of the stream."

"She is, ma'am. And I'd be the happiest man on the water if I marry her. I've come for your blessing."

Ketty gave the foot wheel a sharp kick. "Do you know what happens to a clay vessel if it's fired too soon?"

"No, ma'am."

"It cracks."

"I didn't know that."

"See, if there's a flaw, it won't show up until a mountain of fire's on it. You can never tell until it meets the flames."

"Some pots don't have flaws. They do just fine when heated."

Ketty dipped her hand into a cup of water, then ran it up the length of the clay, narrowing it. "Let's say the potter steps away from a pot and then comes back. That pot needed him the whole time, needed loving hands while it was being formed. If not, it cracks every time."

Wend shifted on his feet. "Dory's favorite mug has a crack on the bottom. He says it holds heat better than any cup he's seen."

"I bet it leaks."

"It doesn't."

Ketty snorted and smashed the pot into a lump. "A man protects his family, above everything."

"That's what my father said."

"But he didn't protect you."

Flames leaped inside Wend, but he contained them. "He was a good man, ma'am. He did the best he could."

With a rag, Ketty began wiping a glove of wet clay from her hand.

"I know what Leena is," said Wend.

Ketty looked up, questioning.

"When I was with the monks, they taught me the Stone Dance. We pretended to step over rocks in the stream, avoiding river snakes and other dangers until at last we found a glistening diamond. That's what Leena is. And I promise I will do everything in my power to keep her safe."

"Leena loves you." Ketty stifled a sob and dabbed her eyes with a kerchief plucked from her bodice. "I won't fight her. She's stubborn enough to wear me down until I consent."

Wend laughed. "I'd rather face a storm."

She wagged her finger at him, but now she was smiling. "Just make sure your best is good enough."

"Yes, ma'am, I will. I know it's hard. If she were my daughter, it would tear me up to part with her. I promise, we'll keep you near."

As she sat under the umbrella patting her eyes, her little clay earrings shaking to and fro, Ketty seemed small and fragile.

❖

Leena *was* a many-faceted diamond. She insisted on making their wedding clothes from the finest loomed fabric. The cloth seemed far too expensive, but Wend offered his fishing money and to sell his canoe.

"You hollowed that canoe through a cold winter," she replied. "You're not selling it. Besides, that merchant is trying to skin me." She proceeded to grind the man into the ground until he threw up his hands and she got her price.

Wend loved watching Leena work on the wedding gown. "Your hands are magic," he said one evening.

"Good. I need it." She laughed. "When I'm old and gray, maybe you'll remember me in this dress."

"The whole village will remember you in it."

"Except Jula."

Leena had known Jula almost as long as she had known Wend, and the two girls had played together as children. She ate but never seemed to put on weight. Her feet were overly large, her ankles bony, and her windpipe protruded from her neck, making her appear more starved than she was.

Jula had a sarcastic sense of humor, and Wend decided that must be what attracted the two girls to each other. But as Wend and Leena's relationship heated up, Jula soured.

"Why is she jealous of you?" Wend asked.

"My sweet innocent. Don't you know how hard it is for a girl like Jula? Her parents dead. No prospects for a husband. If her brother hadn't taken her in, she'd have no boat, only a log to clutch on to. She's completely exposed. The stream would swallow her."

Leena finished the dress and began working feverishly on Wend's suit. Two weeks before the wedding, Jula was stricken with fever. Leena went every day to Jula's boat, bringing broth or medicinal teas. Each day, Jula refused to see her. Leena was just as stubborn. She did Jula's chores and then sat and talked with Jula's brother for an hour.

Early in their courtship, Leena took Wend to evening dances. Paper lanterns were hung over the stage in the market. A violin, two guitars, and a drum played in one corner. It was here that Wend met Leena's friends, among them, Purlo.

"You're alive," Wend cried on first seeing his friend. He lifted Purlo off his feet and hugged him.

"When did you get bigger than me?" Purlo laughed.

"How did you escape Nick and Daggitt?"

"I stole a raft that first night. I tried to get to you, but the current was too strong and swept me downstream."

"I wonder what happened to them."

The lanterns flickered in the warm summer wind. Purlo glanced at them. "Speak of the devil and he'll come." He laughed, but his face paled. "I know what happened to them."

"How?"

"I set up camp where one of the tributaries joined the stream, hoping my uncle would come down that way after he built his boat."

"And he did."

"Yes. He told me he'd organized a band of men to find the pirates who'd been looting and killing. They followed Daggitt and Nick back one night, broke up the camp, and adopted the children. But Nick and Daggitt slipped away downstream."

A week before the wedding, Leena was frantic to finish Wend's suit. He and Purlo watched her put her needles away in a box, and then grab a basket of food she had prepared for Jula.

"The way she's treating you, why do you bother?" Purlo asked.

"Friends don't leave in rough water," Leena replied.

"At least take the suit," said Wend.

Leena packed the suit and her sewing supplies into another basket, and Wend escorted her to Jula's boat.

"I'll walk you home tonight," he said.

"No. I'm staying."

"All night?!"

"As long as it takes."

The next morning, Wend found Leena beside Jula's bed, spooning soup into her friend's mouth.

The suit was done.

Chapter Fourteen

Willow

Wend and Leena married beneath the spreading almond tree. A few days later, they set sail, with Dory and Leena's parents following at a respectful distance.

They glided as in a dream, floating in a mosaic of autumn leaves. Shared with Leena, an apple, a bird, or a simple meal of fish and flatbread became extraordinary.

Time drifted . . .

Snow was velvet on the shores and cotton on the trees . . .

Sun showers dappled the water. Daffodils awakened and painted the hillsides . . .

When peaches fell syrupy from the trees, Willow was born.

From the first, she and Wend were inseparable. After nursing, she napped in Wend's arms. He played with her for hours. Moving a piece of wood beneath a blue blanket, he would say, "The boat's underwater. Can you find it?" Willow giggled and pointed to where the boat poked from the blanket's edge.

He carried her everywhere — to the forest to gather mushrooms, nuts, and berries, or to the shore to fish.

Ketty would shake her head and say, "There's going to be trouble from that. She should be with her mother."

"She cries when she's not with him," Leena replied. "I haven't the heart to separate them."

Ketty promised Wend he would be exhausted from child rearing. Perhaps he was, but he was only aware of excitement, and not wanting to miss anything Willow did. He loved to hear her coo. And to hear her cry. It was a good, strong cry. A cry that shouted to the world, "I'm here, and I'm not going away." That made Wend smile with satisfaction. A cry like that would not be drowned out. It demanded a life. One needed a spirit like that to survive the stream.

Wend built a portable playpen they could take into the forest. "I don't want to be apart from you and Willow," he told Leena. Together, he and Leena gathered fruit, roots, and herbs, and if they were lucky, they trapped a rabbit. When he needed to fish, Leena came down to the stream and made baskets and watched Willow to make sure she was safe.

As soon as she walked she ran and was into everything. Wend had to put latches on all the built-ins.

But a boat is a boat. She tipped over baskets, got tangled in rope, and tumbled across the deck.

Scrapes, scabs, cuts, and bruises ran up her arms and legs. Almost daily, she had to be fished from the water. Not that she didn't already swim like a minnow. She did. But no child was safe unattended on the stream.

If Wend left the boat to hunt, Willow tried to follow. If he was building a fire, she wanted to add sticks. Her interest in Wend's work didn't wane as she grew. One morning, they had moored the boat in a quiet cove. Wend sat beside the shore, chipping blades from a stone. Willow found two stones of her own and tried to chip a knife. Wend took the stones away and told her, "When you're older."

Willow folded her arms. "I can do it."

"But can you do this?" Wend picked up two stones and rang them together. "Find me two that sound like that."

"I can find the best best *best* rocks," cried Willow, and ran in search of them.

By age three, she could tie tackle onto a fishing pole. She knew where to look for bait and had her own little bait jar. Her favorite toys were a boat, a fishing pole, and small wooden fish. She paraded around the boat with these, crying, "I can fish!"

The Stream

A month before her fourth birthday, Willow was sitting on Wend's lap while he fished off the side of the boat.

"Let me hold it," she said, and tried to grab the rod from his hands.

Wend let her hold the handle but folded his hands on top of hers.

"I can do it," she said, trying to wrench her hands away.

"When you're stronger," he said with laugh. "Then you can fish all you want, and I'll sleep in the hammock."

"I'm strong enough."

"You're very strong," he replied, "but not strong enough for a river snake. He'll pull you into the water."

Willow abandoned her toys and began picking up Wend's fishing pole every chance she could. He had to watch like a hawk, or she would snatch up the pole and cast the line.

He and Leena consulted Ketty, who said, "The only thing that worked with you was to send you to the cabin."

"And that not too well." Leena laughed.

But they did as her mother suggested and sent Willow to the cabin when she picked up the pole.

Willow began sneaking out before anyone awakened, so Wend raised the latch on the cabin door. The next morning, he found a chair by the door and

Willow standing by the boat's rail, dropping the fishing line into the water. He raised the latch higher and locked his rod and tackle in a chest.

That did the trick, and for the next few weeks, Willow seemed to forget about fishing. The family was preparing for her *swim*, a rite that coincided with her birthday and marks a child's ability to swim twenty feet alone.

Two days before the ceremony, Dory and Leena's parents joined them to help set up. They were moored in a shady cove. The water was deep, and strangely quiet. Fish should have been plentiful, and fowl too, in the dense foliage beyond the banks.

Dory fished from the side of the boat. He pulled up his line, removed soggy grass from the hook, and recast. "I don't like it," he said. "Fish should be jumping."

"We'll get something," Wend replied.

"We should move on." Dory peered intently into the water. "This isn't a good place."

Wend watched Leena help Willow hang flowering plants around the boat. "It's peaceful here," he said. "I've never seen Willow this calm."

By that evening, Wend wondered if Dory was right. Neither of them had caught a fish, and Wend's traps, scattered in the woods, were empty.

He rose early and cast his line, but by midmorning he still hadn't caught anything.

"Maybe we should head downstream," he said to Leena. "The party can wait."

Leena clapped flatbread dough between her hands. "Willow's been looking forward to this for weeks. It would break her heart."

"We have to eat."

"We'll be fine. I have dried fish, and enough nuts, vegetables, and fruit for ten."

Wend brushed a swatch of flour from Leena's cheek and kissed it. "You're a miracle."

Leena scooped flour from a bowl. She began sprinkling it on her board, but paused and looked at her hand. "Not such a miracle. My ring just fell into the flour."

"Better find it." Wend laughed. "Or someone will break a tooth."

Leena plunged her hand to the wrist in the flour and searched. "Hush. Here it is."

Wend took Leena's shoulders and turned her to him. "You're not eating enough. We should leave."

She shoved him back playfully. "Go back to your fishing, Mr. Wend, and leave the food to me."

Dory arrived next morning with something wrapped in burlap and tied at the top.

"What's in the sack?" asked Wend.

"Fowl," Dory replied. "Only the best for my goddaughter."

"You caught fowl?"

"In a manner of speaking."

Wend gazed at the sack, suspicion growing in his mind. "You didn't . . ." Wend pulled up Dory's sleeves, revealing red marks on his forearms.

"He had it coming."

"We kept him for all these years . . ." Wend replied. "Things won't be the same without him."

"They'd be a sight better for me — if I had killed him. Then I wouldn't have to listen to that cockeyed crow."

"You didn't kill him?"

"I picked him up by the legs and held him upside down to show him who was boss."

"Looks like he got his revenge."

"Never you mind." Dory held up the sack. "I got a dozen eggs. We can use them for a treasure hunt."

Two ropes marked the twenty-foot lane of Willow's swim. Willow was at one end with Leena. Wend waited at the opposite end. The lack of fish had sent two neighboring families downstream, but three remained, and along with Dory and Leena's parents, they were positioned along the length of the ropes for safety. The water was four feet deep, languid, and cool in the summer heat.

Willow had three challenges. First, she rolled onto her tummy with her head in the water. Everyone counted, calling out numbers as if they were playing hide-and-seek and they were all it. Willow was still submerged at twenty seconds, so Leena coaxed her up, giggling and streaming with water.

"I can do more," cried Willow. "Watch me!"

She tried to roll back into the water, but Leena stopped her. "I know, Sweetie, but can you roll and swim to Daddy?"

"Here I come, come, come," Willow called to Wend.

She swam face down a few feet, rolled on her back for a breath, and then swam a few feet. She rolled and swam little by little until she splashed laughing into Wend's arms. He lifted her from the stream, swung her playfully to and fro, and kissed her forehead.

"Am I a good swimmer, Daddy?"

"The best, best, best." Wend laughed and kissed her again about her face and neck until she screamed with delight. "Do you need to rest before swimming to Mommy?"

"Never, never, never," Willow replied, slapping the stream and spraying water with each word.

She turned and swam back to Leena as sleek as a fish.

"I can go again, Mommy. I'm never tired."

Willow turned to go back to Wend, but Leena stopped her. "I know, Sweetie. You could swim all day."

❖

Blue currents undulated above Willow's head, but they weren't the waters of the stream. Leena had tied streamers, dyed a deep azure, to trees near the shore. A breeze sent the streamers out in slow-motion waves. Willow's hair billowed, and Wend had the sensation that she floated underwater and time had stopped. Her black eyes caught the sun like polished obsidian. Her mouth opened to laugh. Her little hands gripped the edge of a burlap sack, her brow crinkled with the challenge of hopping down the lane of streamers with six screaming children.

Wend wished he could hang on to the moment, but Willow was bouncing in her sack, hair flying behind. She pulled ahead of the other children and plunged across the finish line.

Leena had boiled and painted Dory's eggs and hidden them in a roped-off clearing. Willow and her friends dashed from tree to tree and foraged in tall grass and shrubbery, until all the eggs were found. One little boy sank to the dirt and cried because he hadn't found any. Willow gave him her two eggs. He wiped his nose and his eyes looked up at her as if she were a water fairy.

Wend came up behind Leena and wrapped her in his arms. "Just like you were . . . casting her spell."

Leena laughed. "She'll break a few hearts."

Willow pulled the boy up. A moment later another boy was blindfolded, spun in a circle, and the children sang, "River Snake, River Snake, you're alive, you're alive, on the count of five. One, two, three, four, five."

They giggled and shrieked through half a dozen more games, stopping only to stuff their mouths with triangles of flatbread smothered in blackberry jam. Then, licking their fingers, they rushed off to fish prizes from an old sail spread out like the stream.

The day ended as Wend hoped, with Willow passed out from exhaustion. She lay in his arms, with Leena nestled beside him on the deck of their boat. The sunset was mirrored in the stream, where it glowed.

Leena pulled a woolen blanket over them. "How can it blaze during the day and get so cold at night?"

"I don't think I could ever feel anything but warm," replied Wend. He snuggled closer to Leena and inhaled. Willow's hair, soft against his chin, smelled of leaves and the stream. Her breath was a whisper.

The sky deepened. Crickets serenaded in the reeds lining the shore. Neighbors lit lanterns on their boats, casting gold and amber on the water.

"We better get her in bed," Leena whispered.

A memory floated up. On Wend's wedding night, a day bird sang in a tree outside their window. It didn't seem to want the day to end. Or else it sang for the joy of it.

❖

It's going to be a hot day, Wend thought. Shirt-stick-to-your-back hot, as Dory called it. The light was bright, almost painful, behind Wend's eyelids.

Too bright—

His eyes flared. A rectangle of sunlight fell on the cabin floor. Beyond, the door stood open. He turned to look at Willow's bed. The covers were pulled aside. The bed was empty.

The impulse seized Wend to fling his blankets aside, rouse Leena, and dart up the stairs. But Willow had left the cabin, unsupervised, before. He slipped quietly from the covers and crossed the floor, gearing himself up for the sharp scolding he would give her, which hurt him more than it hurt her. Worse was the look on her face when he would send her to the cabin for the rest of the day.

A chorus of frogs croaked nearby. He loved listening to them at night under the stars. But this was morning, and unusual. For the first time they sounded ugly, almost mocking.

Wend crept up the stairs, trying to convince himself that nothing was wrong. He would find her smiling impishly at him, playing with a toy, or her face smeared with jam.

Instinct told him otherwise.

The frogs now sounded like a warning, and a tight band constricted his chest.

He reached the deck. He didn't see her aft. What he did see froze his heart. The chest where he kept his fishing gear was open. The key, which he had hidden, was sitting nearby. Rope, hammer, saw, adze, and knife were still in the chest. The fishing rod and tackle were gone.

He whirled to look behind. Willow was not on the boat.

"Leena!" he shouted.

He rushed to one side of the boat. The water was placid. He could see several feet down. Then it became murky. He needed to see to the bottom. To see if Willow was there.

In a flash, he took in the shoreline. The rocks were bare. The beach was empty. One of the streamers from the party had torn loose on one side. The other side was coiled around a branch. The willow trees leaned toward the stream, as if they wished to touch the water. No wind stirred the reeds.

Only the frogs croaking—

He heard a light splash on the other side of the boat. He rushed across the deck. His breath rasped in his lungs. The boat pounded like a deep, hollow drum beneath his feet. He leaned over the railing. The fishing rod was floating in the water. The fishing line bobbed gently beside it.

"Leena! Leena!"

He heard running up the cabin steps. He swung over the railing. The water was shockingly cold. He dived. Visibility was only a few feet. He couldn't see the bottom. Then he could. He searched left and right. He didn't see Willow. His feet stirred up a confusion of silt. He swam along the bottom, fearful of what he would find.

Willow was strong. She loved that fishing rod. She would be frightened of losing Daddy's rod. She would hold on. Stubborn Willow would hold on.

Wend's lungs seared like hot coals. He kicked off the riverbed and swam up. Turbulence to his right turned him. Leena knifed through the water. He broke the surface, gasping. He dived again. He swam along the bottom, careful not to stir up silt, swimming in an ever-widening arc.

Starving for air, he returned to the surface. He looked for some sign of Willow, in vain hope that she had escaped. Only the waves he and Leena had made rocked the otherwise placid stream.

He dived again, streaking through the water, bubbles streaming from his mouth, fragile worlds that burst on his straining hands, and then he reached the bottom and whipping right and left searched through the tangled confusion of waterweeds for a flash of black hair, a flash of black eyes, eyes that were guilty, angry, or frightened, eyes that were anything but glassy and still. He would have stayed, swimming through the chaos of silt and hydrilla, but his lungs betrayed him and he kicked off the bottom, still searching the murky depths as he rose, mouth clamped to fend off the urge to breathe and gulp water, until at last, his arms and legs as heavy as anchors, he broke the surface.

The water, which had been icy, felt like hot blood. For a moment he saw red. Then his vision cleared. As hot as it seemed, what he saw now chilled him to the bone. Far downstream, barely disturbing the placid surface, a silvery back rolled — scales flashing in the sun — and then it snaked back into the water.

Wend started to swim after it. Leena was beside him now and locked her arms around his.

"It's too late," she cried.

"I have to try!"

"If you follow, you won't be able to come back. I won't lose you too."

Chapter Fifteen

The Shaggy Man

Wend drifted.

Except for odd moments, the world was a vague impression seen through a scrim. Color faded. The song of the stream, the trill of birds were lost.

Dory had been barking at him for days. "Look sharp! We're in shallow waters."

At those moments, Wend looked around as if he had awakened from a trance. His boat would be veering toward rocks or the shore, and he would right his course.

He preferred trapping and hunting to fishing, but fish were the mainstay on the stream, and duck, geese, and rabbit had become scarce. He fished with his net when he could, but results were unreliable. When it was fish or die, he picked up his rod and stared at it, barely feeling it in his hands, aware only of the tears rolling down his cheeks and into the water.

Dory and Leena's parents took over the evening meals, making flatbread, stews, and casseroles in an effort to give the couple relief. Wend often excused himself, sat alone near the bow, and stared at the stream.

At night, he and Leena lay in each other's arms and cried.

On one such night, she whispered, "I'm going to pack Willow's things."

"Her little toys?" The toys held a piece of Willow. To move them was unthinkable. They belonged where she had dropped them. They waited for her.

"Seeing them is too hard," Leena replied. "For both of us."

The next day, she walked around the boat with a large basket and collected Willow's dolls, marbles, tops, puppets, and other toys. Then she went into the cabin, shut the door, and Wend heard her sobbing.

He gripped the tiller and stared at the cabin door. He could hear her shutting the windows and moving things.

Part of him wanted to rush down and stop her. What she was doing was wrong. Nothing of Willow's should be touched. But Leena had turned and looked at him fiercely, her bloodshot eyes seeming to say, *Don't follow. Don't try to stop me.*

Dory sounded as if he was shouting from deep inside a long tunnel. At first, Wend could not understand the words. He clutched the tiller, but he was in the cabin with Leena, watching her fold Willow's bedding and stow it in a drawer, collect her cup, baby fork, and spoon, wrap them in soft cloth, and then place them at the bottom of a basket. Then the basket was pushed to the back of storage deep within the prow.

The urgency in Dory's voice sharpened. The words broke through. "Look out!"

Wend's boat was flying straight toward a sandbar. He turned the rudder. The boat was going too fast. It ran up on the bar with a sick sound—as if a thousand frogs shrieked in its belly.

Wend leaped to the ground, fearing timber had peeled from the hull. By the time he had circled the boat, Leena was leaning over the rail and her parents and Dory had pulled up in their boats, as close as they dared.

"Are you all right?" Wend called to Leena.

"Just tell me the boat is okay." Leena climbed off the boat and walked around it with Wend.

The boat was sound, but it was stuck on the shoal like a fly in tree sap. Only the stern remained in the water. The whole family tried pushing it back into the stream, but it wouldn't budge.

The Stream

Wend leaned against the hull, catching his breath. "What do I do?" he asked Dory.

Dory lit his pipe and studied the boat. "Leave it."

Desperation rose in Wend's throat. "I can't do that."

Dory sent up a cloud of blue-white smoke. "Then wait for the stream to lift it."

"There's got to be a way! People will come along and help us."

"We needed the whole village to launch it," Dory replied. "We haven't seen that many people for months."

Wend turned to climb back onto the boat.

Leena gripped his arm and pointed across the stream. "We can stay there."

Wend took in the scene at a glance, the almost still water, the cliff wall, as red as dried blood, rising forty feet like an imposing fortress. Erosion and a natural groove formed a rough set of steps up the cliff. Beyond, a solitary cabin sat on a patch of land. Beyond that, alien trees loomed like an invading army.

"No." Pulling away, he started climbing onto the boat.

"We have to," she called after him.

On the boat, Wend flung his tools aside, grabbed his shovel, and stormed back to the spit.

"Wend, for the love of all that's sane," cried Leena, "what are you doing?"

Holding the shovel in both hands, Wend slammed the blade into the gravelly earth. "I'm digging my way out."

"Won't work," said Dory.

Wend ignored him, sending sand, pebbles, and small stones flying.

Dory put a restraining hand on Wend's arm. "Even if you dig out the whole boat, the water level's too low. You'll never move it."

Wend wrenched away and thrust the shovel into the ground with his foot.

Leena lashed him with a blaze of oaths and curses that would have made a pirate quail. Wend was as immovable as the boat.

"Leave him be," Dory said to her. "He'll find out soon enough."

Wend dug away, vaguely aware that Leena and the rest of the family packed clothes, blankets, cups, and plates and moved them ashore in Wend's canoe.

Late that night, his hands swollen and blistered, he tossed the shovel aside, leaned against the boat, and pushed. "Move. Move, damn you!"

He began kicking the boat, his screams echoing off the rock walls on both sides of the stream.

The clatter of cooking pots roused Wend from a dreamless slumber. His hands throbbed. Every muscle felt as if it had been pummeled. He burrowed deep into his furs in a vain attempt to return to the anesthesia of sleep.

Ketty and Skip talked softly ten, fifteen feet away. The cooking fire popped, then settled into a steady crackle. The aroma of salted pork penetrated the covers pulled over Wend's head.

Fatigue battled hunger. Fatigue would have won, but Leena whispered, "Are you awake? Breakfast is ready."

"Let me be," he grumbled.

"Your eggs will get cold." He heard a plate clink softly on a nearby rock, and then her footsteps returning to the fire.

Wend groaned and tried to slip back into sleep, wishing the numbness he felt inside would spread to his muscles.

He hid under the blanket a good hour, would have stayed all day, but Leena returned.

"I need your help," she said.

He crawled from the blankets. She handed him a steaming mug of tea and his eggs. He sat on a hollowed-out log, eating slowly, holding the mug in a piece of cloth to protect his blisters.

Wind nipped at his neck as he surveyed his surroundings. The ground from the cliff edge to where he sat was rock—red and barren but for a few weeds trembling in the cracks. The rock gave way to hardpan on which the lone cabin had been built.

Dory came up and sat beside him. "I hope you're satisfied," he said, glancing at Wend's hands.

"You could have helped." Wend eyed the narrow path that led from the cabin up a slope to the trees. The branches, waving in the wind, seemed to beckon him.

"No sense having four useless hands." Dory nodded toward Leena, who was drying a pot. "She's being a saint. Don't push it. She won't take it forever."

"What are you talking about?"

"If you keep this up, you'll lose her."

Wend stared at his mug, where steam was clinging to the edge before evaporating into the morning chill.

Dory rose. "If you were a kid again, I'd tan your hide. You're not the only one hurting."

What scared Wend was that he didn't care.

While he had been digging, the family had spent the day unloading the three boats. Leena had insisted they camp the first night so she could give the cabin a good scrubbing. Now she pulled Wend inside. The cabin was empty, save for tattered curtains, a cracked wooden bowl, and a burned pot that a line of ants marched around. The windows were empty eye sockets, shuttered tightly. Dust had settled on the interior like a blanket of snow.

"I'm not staying here," Wend said.

"Fine," replied Leena, "but you'll help me clean it." She banged one of the shutters open with Dory's mallet. "Well, what are you waiting for?"

Wend walked out of the cabin and into the trees.

Leena had the cabin shipshape by the end of the first day. Wend refused to enter.

Her eyes flashed, a sure sign a storm was brewing. "Why won't you come in?"

"The wood's rotten."

"Only one piece of the floor. Dory fixed it."

Leena tugged him to the doorway. Yellow curtains fluttered in the windows. Table, chairs, and a round sienna-colored rug from the boat formed a cozy nook beside the hearth. A blaze of fall lay on the table, where an orange tablecloth, a bowl of gourds, and a pitcher of dried maple leaves were arranged.

Wend took one sniff, turned on his heel, and stalked into the woods.

The first week, Wend spent his nights camped beneath the stars. Leena asked him why he wouldn't come inside.

"It smells moldy," he replied.

During the day, he couldn't bear to go near the stream, where the boat loomed like a castaway. Instead, he retreated to the forest with his ax over his shoulder. The trees were massive, almost noble, but for the bark, which was peeling and torn. Purple sap, so dark it was nearly black, oozed from the exposed wood.

He attacked the trees, swinging his ax relentlessly, mindless that he broke open his blisters.

Numbness started at his head and worked down his body, inch by inch, until it felt as if someone else chopped and Wend was but a ghost.

The solitude of the trees drew him. The shadows were deep. The branches, woven tightly, left only small windows to the sky. Save for the stroke of his ax, all was silent, though sometimes he thought he heard worms chewing the carpet of dead leaves.

One day, he stopped chopping to mop his brow with his sleeve, and found Dory standing at the edge of the clearing, staring at him.

"Have enough wood there?" Dory asked.

Wend looked around, seeing for the first time the flotsam of trees, logs, and chips strewn across the clearing, as if a colossal flood had knocked down the trees and scattered them. "I'll build something with it."

Dory snorted. "It's worthless. Too brittle to do anything with."

"Then it's firewood." Wend picked up his ax and swung it into a block of wood, cleaving it in two. "Do you smell anything strange?"

"Just you. You haven't bathed in days. You planning a beard?"

Wend stopped chopping and felt the rough growth on his cheek, absently. "Mold. That's what I'm smelling."

Dory sniffed. "Just tree sap."

"No. It's mold."

That night, he slept in the cabin.

Leena snuggled up to him beneath the furs. "See?" she whispered. "All clean in here. No mold."

"There is," he replied. "I like it."

It was neither day nor night, but that twi-time after sunset when trees and mountains dim to specters. Wend leaned his ax near the cabin door and entered. The walls flickered from the hearth fire—the only source of illumination—and for a moment Wend had the sensation he was inside the Pavilion.

Thrust into mittens, Leena's hands looked misshapen as she pulled a roasting pot from the fire. Skip talked quietly with Dory. They exchanged glances when Wend entered. Ketty sat at a small table near one of the windows, working on a paper puzzle Leena had made by cutting up a painting.

"Wash up, Sweetie," said Leena. "Dinner's ready."

Wend looked at his hands. The nails had grown long. Dirt formed dark crescent moons above the quick. Dirt and wood dust ran up his hands and arms like the pattern of a map.

He drew out his chair at the dinner table and sat. Ketty, a few feet away at the puzzle, stiffened.

"Pig," she said, under her breath. She moved her chair to the other side of her table and returned to the puzzle.

Dory and Skip joined Wend.

"Could you lend me hand a tomorrow, Wend?" asked Skip. "I'm replacing that old railing."

Wend stared at the threads in the tablecloth, noticing the tiny shadows between stitches. "I'm busy."

Dory cursed. "Doing nothin'."

"I'm chopping wood."

"You got enough for two winters." Dory gazed at Wend's arms and shoulders. "The only thing you're getting out of it is stronger. A lot stronger."

"I don't feel strong . . ."

Leena brought a platter to the table. Small potatoes and baked apples, glistening in juice, were arranged around the edge. Something sat in the center, with toasted pecans sprinkled on top. But that *thing* beneath the nuts — roughly triangular, pale, pinkish white, bones through the center . . .

"What is this?" asked Wend.

"Don't be silly." Leena laughed. With a spatula, she fixed Wend's plate and set it in front of him.

He stared at the food a moment, then picked up his fork and began pushing the potatoes and apples away from the *thing*.

Leena sat and reached out to Ketty. "Join us."

Ketty glanced at Wend, and then leaned over the puzzle. "No thanks."

"Well, I'm starving." Leena dived into her food.

Wend ate around the *thing*.

When half of her food was eaten, Leena came up for air and looked at Wend's plate. "Is something wrong? Don't you like it?" she asked him.

"What is it?" he replied.

Leena stifled a sob. "It's your favorite."

He finished the apples and potatoes, trying to ignore the growing horror on Leena's face, and pushed the plate away.

Ketty glared at him. "It's a sin to waste food from the water."

"I don't know what it is," said Wend.

"It's f—sh, you big oaf," she replied.

Wend sprang back, as if a hissing snake were coiled in the dish. His chair crashed into the puzzle table. The pieces fluttered to the floor, jumbled.

Later that evening, Wend stood outside the door, looking up at the stars, bright pinpoints that were, with the sun and moon, the only constants in his life.

Beneath the chirping crickets and the occasional sensation that worms were crawling through eons of decayed vegetation, he heard the family whispering.

Leena cried softly. "What do I do?"

"*I'll* tell you what you do," said Ketty. "You pack up and leave him."

"*Never,*" Leena replied.

"If you don't," said Ketty, "you'll end up as crazy as he is. He'll turn your life to hell."

"Hush, Mother," said Skip. "He's a good lad. He'll snap out of it."

"He won't," said Ketty. "I've seen it before. Shaggy men with vacant eyes."

"Aye," said Dory, "I've seen it too."

"He's gone," said Ketty. "You have to accept that."

"I won't," said Leena, vehemently. "Dory, you must know a way."

A puff of aromatic smoke wafted out the door. "It's a strange kind of sickness. Never saw a cure," said Dory.

"Dory, *please.*" Leena's voice sounded strained, as if a rope had tightened around her neck.

Two long puffs of silver floated out the door. "He's been avoiding the str—m. Take him there tomorrow."

Str—m . . . Wend's mind clouded at the strange word. Just as it had when Ketty said f—sh to describe the thing on his plate.

A while later, the candles went out. Leena came outside, hooked her arm around Wend's, and laid her head against his shoulder. They stood quietly, watching the stars.

He didn't ask what the strange words meant. Better to stuff them away, as they had Willow's things.

Next morning, Wend tried to sneak out early. He was halfway from the covers when Leena wrapped her arms around his waist.

"Wait," she said. "I need you for something."

"Later." He tried to pull away, but she held tight.

"No. Now." Her face hardened with the look she had turned on the fabric merchant.

The rest of the family rolled from their bedclothes and escorted Wend outside.

The sun was bright, the air cold and bracing. High above, an eagle circled in the cloudless blue. The tree line, no thinner for all of Wend's chopping, marched down toward the barren rock, glistening with dew.

"I need to work," he said.

"Soon," she replied. "I want to show you something."

He felt the pressure of her hand on his arm, turning him. The rock sloped down to swirling fog.

"Strange weather," he said. "There's a blanket of fog."

Leena gasped.

Dory took his other arm. "Take him down to it."

They led him across the rock and down into the fog, which undulated and twisted, and then he realized it wasn't fog at all, but a blurry space in his vision, as if he were trying to peer into a pond agitated by rain.

Leena still held his arm. "Look, Sweetie. The str—m."

"The what?" he replied.

"And your b—t." Leena's fingers tightened on his arm. "Don't you see it?"

"No."

"Take him to the water," said Dory.

They guided him down the groove in the cliff wall to a narrow shelf.

"Tell me you see it," Leena cried.

Wend shuffled, uncertain what he should see. Part of him knew he should be alarmed, but he felt only indifference, and he wished to get back to his ax, logs, and chopping, accompanied by the sound of chewing worms.

She gripped his arm like a vice and shook it. "Tell me you see it!" Letting go of his arm, she squatted, reached down into the blurry space, and her hands disappeared up to her wrists. She withdrew them cupped with water. "Remember? Remember now?!"

He stared at the glistening pool in her hands. "It's magic."

The water drained from her fingers.

Later that day, he said to Leena, "Strange—at the bottom of the cliff is a field."

❖

Next morning, Dory followed Wend outside and asked him for help building a new wing on the cabin. "We could get it done before winter."

"I'm busy," Wend replied. "Loan me your pick."

Dory's eyes narrowed. "What for?"

"Digging."

Dory stared at Wend a moment, cursed, and stalked off behind the cabin, where he kept his tools. He returned with a pick and handed it to Wend.

Leena had parceled off a small plot near the cabin where she managed to squeeze out some stunted peas and cabbage. Wend chose a spot just beyond her garden and began cracking open hardpan where a few weeds had taken hold.

Dory cradled his pipe in one hand and watched, a wry smile curling his lips. "What do you hope to get out of that?"

Wend swung the pick, feeling the impact up his arms, grateful to feel anything beyond his usual numbness. "A well."

"You won't find a drop. The only thing you're digging is your grave." Dory nodded toward the field. "Why don't you try down there?"

Wend ignored him. Leena's hands had disappeared there. The field was suspicious territory, and he didn't like the strange murmur he heard there. Maybe the place was haunted.

He dug until he hit bedrock. The next morning, he chose another spot, and labored all day until his pick rang on stone. He moved his efforts closer to tree line, where the soil ran deep with the roots of the trees. By the end of fall, the ground between the garden and the trees was honeycombed with holes.

Wend trudged into the cabin one evening and slouched into his chair.

"Maybe I'm not digging deep enough," he said to Dory.

"Give it up," Dory replied. "There's no water down there."

"There's got to be," Wend cried. "We'll die without water."

Leena came up behind him. Running her fingers through his hair — grown long and shaggy — she worked at the knots. "Hush," she said. "I always find water."

The fact that Leena found water for drinking, cooking, and cleaning was a vague notion hidden behind clouds, a mystery best left alone, like the field.

Ketty, hunched over a puzzle, flung down one of the pieces. "Why are you humoring him?"

"Mother, we talked about this," said Leena, sharply.

"He's ruining you." Ketty's voice clanged like metal pots.

Wend stuffed his fingers in his ears, jerked to his feet, and hurried outside. Loud sounds hurt his ears.

His hearing had become sensitive. Why else would he hear the worms? Or ghosts whispering in the field. . . .

He sank onto the hollow log, some distance from the cabin, hearing every word of the argument.

"You will *not* talk about my husband that way."

"We're all walking on eggshells," Ketty shouted. "Tell him the truth, girl."

"It would crush him. He needs time."

"His mind is busted. Nothing heals that."

"He'll snap out of it."

"Damn stubborn girl—he'll destroy you. I'm sorry I ever let him near you. I should have sent him back to the monks—"

(for a moment, Wend's brain clouded)

" —but you never could resist stray dogs."

Leena began crying. "Everyone on the str—m is a stray."

"Throw him in—let him sink or swim."

"Whatever happened to 'Our home is your home'?"

"I can't take this anymore." (Wend could picture Ketty holding her head in her hands.) "I swear, I'll leave."

Leena's voice snapped like a whip. "There's the door."

Wend gave up digging for water. Instead, he rose early each morning and searched for bark to beat into fiber. Then, with fiber piled around his feet, he spent hours twirling it into string that he spliced end to end until he had coils of it. Occasionally, he looked up from his work and sniffed the air. Colossal clouds, charcoal and oppressive, dwarfed the landscape. Then his fingers flew, and if not for his calluses, they would have bled.

By the first rain, he had woven a basket. When the storm had passed, he rushed out to see the result of his work. Water had collected inside but was leaking swiftly out the sides and bottom.

We'll die of thirst, he thought, and went in search of Leena. He found her behind the cabin, loading laundry into a washtub.

She sighed when she saw him. "What?"

"My basket leaked."

She gave him a tired smile. "A cow could pass through your weave."

"You could do it."

"Who would catch dinner, cook, and clean?" she snapped. Holding up the laundry, she gave it a shake. "Who would do this?"

"But we need to collect water."

"I don't have time for this." She stalked off to the field.

Wend tried to improve his weave and tested it with the next rain. The second basket leaked as much as the first, but beside it was another basket, solid as a jug, that had collected water.

The Stream

He still felt numb daily, but not at that moment. Not for Leena.

She made it, Wend thought. *She made it for me.*

With the rains, the ghosts in the field grew louder. Wend was certain they called to him, trying to draw him into their grasp. Memories floated into his mind, tales he had heard around cooking fires of spirits and fiends who lured the unwary traveler. Once caught, the poor soul was trapped forever.

Wend asked Dory if he believed the tales. Dory shrugged, but Leena's mother muttered under her breath, "You're already caught."

He became convinced spirits watched him through the windows, that they crept inside and stood grinning over him while he slept. Each night, before going to bed, he scattered ashes on the floor. Each morning, he searched for footprints. That he never found the ash disturbed only confirmed their power.

Sometimes, long after the others were asleep, Wend thought he heard Willow calling to him. Then he slipped from the covers and went into the night, searching for her.

Sometimes, when he was in the forest, the trees seemed to move toward him. He had the same sensation inside the cabin. The walls breathed, in and out; then in, in, in. Fearing he would be crushed, he rushed out the door.

Sometimes, when he returned later, he heard Leena crying, in back of the cabin, never inside, where he would see her. He only saw her cry once. Peeking around the corner of the cabin, he had found her leaning against the wall, turned away from him. Her shoulder rose and fell in almost imperceptible jerks. A washrag dangled from one hand, as if for a moment it had been forgotten.

Wend's foot slid on a pebble. Leena stiffened, wiped her eyes, and, without turning, walked with a straight back down to the field.

Sometimes, later, floating up with the singing of the ghosts, Wend thought he heard her crying from the field.

He wanted to follow, to give her comfort, but sweat, cold and clammy, sprang to his skin, and he hurried into the forest.

After a cold, blinding rain, the ghosts sent wind smelling of mud, and they wailed in a thousand strange tongues. Wend rushed into the trees to get away. Finding peace at last, he kept going straight in one direction, something he had never done before, and plunged deep into the forest. He didn't follow a path. There was none to follow; the forest floor was barren except for centuries of moldering leaves, but the trees grew apart from each other and were easy to pass through. Judging from the sun, he had walked a good hour when he came upon a clearing. Chopped-down trees lay scattered about, and beyond was a cabin.

His cabin.

The next day he tried again, keeping the sun to his left to stay on a straight course. After three miles, he found himself walking again through the clearing toward the cabin.

As he neared the garden, yelling erupted from cabin. If the forest twisted back on itself, there was no escape there. Forward was an argument. He sank down among the stunted peas, defeated.

He heard every word.

"He'll never go there," cried Leena.

"But the b—t is floating," shouted Ketty. "Now's our chance to leave."

"I can't make him."

"Tie him up and drag him."

Leena laughed scornfully. "Who wants to try? Father? Dory?"

"I'd rather tangle with a bear," said Dory.

The next morning, Wend tested the forest again. He walked a straight course in one direction, the sun always to his left. An hour later, he was back where he'd started.

As he left the clearing, he saw Leena walking up the path toward him, a stranger beside her.

Her face was bright. "Wend, look who's here." She smiled, and Wend couldn't remember when he'd last seen one so broad and filled with hope.

Wend studied the stranger, who wore a wide-brim hat that shaded the remnants of peeling sunburn. Straight white hair fanned over his ears.

"Purlo . . ." said Wend.

"You know me, old friend." Purlo grinned.

Wend looked around. "How did you get here?"

Purlo glanced at Leena and shifted his feet, uncertainly. "The usual way . . ."

"Sit and visit," said Leena. "I'll make lunch."

Purlo watched her walk down to the cabin. "She's a good woman."

"Do you know, if you go in one direction in that forest," Wend said, nodding toward the trees, "you always return here?"

Purlo's lips were chapped. He licked them carefully. "Hasn't it always been that way?"

"Really? I had a vague notion about that, but I couldn't put my finger on it."

Purlo took off the hat and turned it in his hands. "Do you remember when we were kids?"

"We were friends."

"Anything more? What we did?"

"No."

"Do I remind you of anything?"

"No. You are you."

Purlo put the hat back on. Picking up a stick, he pressed the point into a groove in the rock, where a bit of earth had collected and a few weeds grew. "I wish I had known Willow. I'm sorry you lost her."

Wend fought the urge to rise. "Sometimes I look for her."

They sat for a long time in silence.

Purlo spent most of his time with Wend, chopping wood, walking in the forest, setting traps that never caught game. He smiled and laughed, even though Wend remained solemn. Except one time, when Purlo said, "That's quite a beard, old friend," Wend chuckled, nodded toward Purlo's clean-shaven face, and said, "You should grow one."

Purlo helped Leena too, and Wend often saw them talking quietly together. Once, as winter waned, Wend came upon Purlo helping her hang laundry to dry. Wend would have stepped away, but he heard his name. They seemed unaware of him leaning against the cabin wall.

"Does he remember anything?" Leena asked.

"Nothing," Purlo replied.

Leena shook out a shirt and pinned it to the clothesline. "Not even our days with Jula and the gang?"

"He knows the names, but everything about the str—m is gone."

"I hoped seeing you would jog his memory."

Purlo hung a shirt on the line, where it fluttered. "How long will you wait?"

"What do you mean?"

"You know what I mean."

"I don't." A note of irritation crept into Leena's voice.

"You're young. Beautiful. Your whole life is before you."

"My life is here."

"You could make another family. Have children."

"This is my family."

"Leena, please, you'll wither here."

She snatched a towel from the basket. As she reached up to pin the towel, the short sleeves of her blouse fell, revealing her shoulders, taut and defined. "If I leave him, then I'm no good."

Dory said the damn rocks outside were hot enough to bake flatbread. No one tried it. Mosquitoes and a blasting sun kept the family inside.

No fowl, rabbit, or squirrel had been seen in months. Because there was nothing else, Wend ate the strange pink meat that Leena tried to hide in soups and casseroles. As the days lengthened, the portions on his plate shrank.

The Stream

"Another sweat-stick-to-your-back day," said Dory one afternoon. "Since we're all here anyway, we better meet."

Leena's father put down a lantern he was making and stepped to the table, where Dory, Purlo, and Wend already sat. Leena joined them, setting down a pitcher of the blackberry juice — thinned with water and sweetened with honey — that she'd been serving all summer.

"You too, Mother," she said.

Ketty was drooping at the puzzle table, fanning herself. "Must I?" she grumbled.

Dory pointed at her with the stem of his pipe. "It concerns you as much as the rest of us." He waited until she pulled out of her chair and flopped into another at the table. Then he began dropping threads of tobacco into his pipe. "No use dodging it. We all know. We're running out of food."

Ketty folded her arms. "We need to leave. Find a different spot."

Wend watched a mosquito land on his arm. He waited until it started boring before brushing it away. "We can't leave. We can't go more than three miles. I tried it."

Ketty snorted. "By the str — m, you fool, the *str — m.*"

"Mother," Leena warned.

Dory dropped in another pinch of tobacco and tamped it down. "Here's the truth. Wend won't leave.

Leena won't leave without him. And we're not pulling enough f—sh to feed all of us. The rest of us have to move on."

"She'll starve," Ketty cried.

"I've been salting f—sh and laying it aside," Dory replied.

"So have I," said Purlo. His face, like all of their faces, had grown gaunt, but it glowed as he gazed at Leena.

"What about that rooster?" Wend asked, suddenly remembering there was a rooster. Sometimes, he even thought he heard him crow, down in the field.

"Now, you wouldn't kill something just cause it's ornery, would you?" Dory replied. "Life wouldn't have no spice without that rooster."

"Not much meat on it anyway." Wend laughed, the sound foreign to his ears.

"When will you go?" Leena asked.

Dory pulled the tobacco from his pipe, thread by thread. "Soon."

Heat waves rising off rock made the world tenuous, as if it would evaporate. The family stood on a level space overlooking the field, as close as Wend would venture. He glanced apprehensively at the grass, which seemed to shimmer and blur with it's own heat.

Purlo hugged Wend tightly. "Take care of her, old friend."

"I'll try," Wend replied.

Purlo turned to Leena. "It's not too late. You can come."

"You know I can't."

"He may never come out of it."

"Then we die together. You know how I feel —"

"Friends don't leave in rough water," Purlo said, finishing for her. He slung his pack over his shoulder. "And I'm abandoning you."

She kissed his cheek. "You're making sure we eat." She turned to Ketty, who had been sniveling, but now a cascade of tears came pouring down her face.

"I'll never see you again," she wailed, and threw herself into Leena's arms.

Leena rocked her like a child. "We had to part sometime."

"Not like this. Who'll protect you?"

"We'll be fine."

"You won't. He's worthless. He won't lift a finger to protect you."

Leena straightened. While Skip pulled Ketty away and tried to quiet her, Dory took Wend aside.

"Do you remember the day I told you to float?" Dory asked.

"I remember the words. Not the day."

"You understood the words when you were a boy. Do you understand them now?"

"I don't know."

"Well, think on it. I've done all I can for you. The rest is up to you. Try to take care of her. Hold her soft, hold her tight, but never let her go." Dory wiped his eyes.

"A man does that."

"A man does."

"I remember that."

"Then maybe things will work out." Dory turned away.

"Dory?"

Dory looked back.

"I stayed, didn't I? I stayed a good long while."

"You did, son. You got under my skin good."

The family gathered a few remaining things and began hiking down the groove in the cliff.

Wend stood beside Leena, his gaze on Dory. "Does he know I love him?"

"He knows."

The family reached the edge of the field and faded in the heat waves.

Seasons melted into seasons. There was only day and night, hot and cold. Some days, Wend found himself standing in the rain, and he would have continued standing but for Leena, who would throw a cloak over him and lead him back to the cabin.

The old ghosts left him alone. New ghosts haunted him . . . voices of the family. He was uncertain whether they taunted him from the field or rattled around in his head. It didn't matter. They spoke, and he felt just as invisible as he had when they had lived with him.

"I don't like it. It's all on Leena . . ." cried Purlo.

Ketty wailed, "You may never see any of us again."

Purlo: "It tears me up seeing you like this. I don't know what to do for him. I don't know what any of us can do."

Ketty: "To think that I should see her come to this. Living with *that.*"

Ketty: "You know what the str — m can bring."

Ketty: "He won't lift a finger to protect you."

He bore it all with the vague notion he was being punished for some crime. He lived in a dim, colorless world, where objects were shadows. He wondered if he was still in the Pavilion. If perhaps he had never left it. If everything that had happened afterward had been a dream. And indeed, the cabin walls, the forest, even the world outside seemed to breathe. At times, he feared it would collapse on itself and crush him.

Only Leena's straight back and blue-black hair remained from the old world.

During a period of heat (it must have been summer), the portions on his plate grew smaller. The flash in Leena's eyes faded, replaced by desperation.

They spoke little, days (weeks? months?) going by without a word.

One day, she said, "Come outside. I want to show you something."

She led him to the woodpile behind the cabin. A long object was covered with canvas.

"Take it off," she said, nodding to the canvas.

"What is it?"

"Something you need to see."

Wend hesitated. There was something familiar about the shape. But it was out of place here and might make this world fall in on itself. This world, for all its strangeness, was safe.

"It might help," she urged.

When he made no move, she reached down and pulled off the canvas. The object was made from one block of wood, fifteen by three feet, and hollow so you could sit in it.

Wend staggered back. The object was taboo. A nightmare he wanted to forget. He tried to cover his eyes, as if he were looking at the sun. Dory and Willow flashed into his mind, flickers from an alien world.

He reached for the ax leaning against the wood pile.

"*No!*" Leena shouted. She latched on to his arm. Hung her full weight on it.

He shook her off like a leaf. "It's too terrible," he cried.

"But it's yours!" She ducked away from the ax as he raised it. "You made it. As a boy."

A ghastly oath boiled up and exploded from his lips as the ax struck. "Daggitt!" He swung the ax, again and again. "Daggitt — Daggitt — Daggitt — "

Leena sagged against the woodpile, her face twisted in horror.

When the object was chopped to pieces, he flung them off the cliff, watching them bounce and shatter and tumble into the field. For a moment they seemed to float, held aloft in a strange, swirling pattern. Then they faded into a patch of daisies.

Chapter Sixteen

Gifts

Carrying an armful of firewood, Wend trudged through a blanket of snow, blindingly bright in the midday sun. The sky was clear, the air piercing.

He entered the cabin and found an old man warming his hands by the fire. His shirt and pants were tattered, revealing the muscles beneath, which stood out like cords. He was thin, so thin that Wend could wrap one hand around one of the man's arms.

Leena stirred the contents of a steaming pot. She looked up as Wend strode across the room and set the wood down by the fire.

She smiled at him, the first he'd seen in a long time. "Look, Wend. We have a visitor."

"I won't stay long," the old man said.

"Stay as long as you like," Wend replied. He peeked into Leena's pot. Soup bubbled inside, and the aroma made his stomach rumble. "Is it ready?" he asked her. "I'm starving."

"Ready," she replied. With potholders, she carried the pot to the table.

"Let me help you up, old man," Wend said.

The man was crouching, turning his hands above the flames. "I'm fine." He rose and walked to the table with the step of a younger man.

Leena ladled the meal into clay bowls and served them. Before sitting, Wend took a small bowl of soup and set it outside the door.

"It's good to give something back," said the old man. The wrinkles on his face were deep, like ripples.

"Where did you come from?" asked Wend.

The old man smiled, revealing a chipped front tooth. "Where everyone comes from."

"Your teeth are white."

"From eating f—sh." The man leaned forward, his eyes penetrating. "You know f—sh . . ."

Wend glanced at his soup, where celery root, winter squash, and chunks of pale pink meat floated. "We're eating it."

The man tore a piece of flatbread and sopped up broth from his bowl. He ate the bread slowly, reverently. "The str—m brings gifts. Today it's you."

"And you," Leena replied. "We haven't had company in an age."

Wend was relieved when Leena and the old man slipped into quiet conversation. Since coming to this place, conversation had become difficult for him. He heard the sounds for words like f — sh and str — m, but a cloud obscured their full meaning.

Besides, he wanted to study the old man. There was something familiar about him. The knobby knees . . . the chipped tooth . . .

A memory floated into Wend's mind of another meal, of a bowl traded for a basket, and a gift of fresh water.

"I know you," said Wend, trying to pull together the fragments of the memory.

The old man turned away from Leena. His gaze roamed Wend's face. "Maybe. I get around."

"You asked me a question, twice, long ago . . . don't ask it."

"What question is that?"

"What I want today."

"I don't need to. Something will come and ask it for me."

After lunch, Wend went into the forest to check his traps. When he returned that evening, the old man was gone.

He and Leena made love, the first time since Willow died. The numbness he had been feeling abated . . . and returned with the next storm, a cold, lashing rain. The ghosts roared in the field. Wend felt as if they were cursing him. He ran into the forest to escape their wrath, only to find that the trees had changed. Fungus clung to the trunks and branches like rust. Moss hung like hair from the branches and snaked along the ground. If not for his traps, he would not have left the cabin, but Leena brought little food from the field.

"Can you help me, Wend?" Leena asked one night. Her eyes were hollow sockets; the dark shadows around them frightening. But not as frightening as the ghosts.

"I can't go down there. They'll swallow me up."

Leena ran from the cabin. Wend heard her keening above the wind and the ghosts.

As if in revenge, a bitter storm rose and pelted the cabin with hail. They kept snug by the fire, but only water and a few limp vegetables simmered in the cooking pot.

The first break in the storm, Wend ventured out to check his traps, placed along a three-mile loop around the forest. His boots sank deep into the mud as he slogged from trap to trap. They were empty. Over the months (years?) that he'd kept them, he'd caught a squirrel and a rat. They had eaten the squirrel. He let the rat go.

He was turning homeward when a dozen wild pigs burst through a curtain of moss and charged across his path. He froze, his hand hovering above the knife at his belt. They ran on, their grunts fading away. He exhaled in relief but proceeded with knife in hand.

He checked the traps on the downward loop. They were as empty as his stomach. But inside the third-from-last trap, a rabbit panted.

By the time Leena had the rabbit roasting, cold rain was lashing the cabin. They were about to eat when someone pounded on the door.

Ghosts? Wend wondered. But the ghosts had never been so direct. They mocked him from the field, or crept around the cabin while he slept, scattering ash to cover their footsteps.

Wend opened the door. A hulking figure loomed at the entrance. The wind whipped his slicker. Rain fell in strings from his hat. Beneath the brim, the eyes were cold disks.

Wend ushered him in and took his hat and coat. The man walked to the fire, Wend going along so it appeared that he led the man. But in fact, the man helped himself to the fire. Wend glanced at Leena. Her eyes narrowed.

The man squeezed water from the bottoms of his pants with two huge hands, then straightened and looked around the room, taking in the guitar and flutes Dory had hung on the walls, Leena's cloth wall hangings, and the dinner table—bright and festive with yellow tablecloth, dried flowers, colored gourds, and the steaming rabbit in the center. His gaze stopped on

Wend, traveled quickly up his torso and limbs, and then moved on with a dismissive curl of his lips to Leena, where it lingered on her breasts.

"Please, join us for dinner," she said, breaking the awkward silence. "We have little, but we always share."

The man strode to the table and sat. His ears were small, his jaw square. Gray stubble covered his face like coarse sand. He glanced impatiently at Wend and Leena's places at the table, as if to say, hurry up, let's get started.

Wend and Leena sat quickly, and Wend began carving the rabbit.

"Anyone else live with you?" The man's voice was like gravel.

"No," Wend replied, serving the man slices of rabbit. Wend cut portions for Leena and himself. Putting a small piece of meat in the offering bowl, he left it outside the door.

"You're wastin' it," the man said when Wend had reseated himself.

Wend glanced at Leena. She avoided the man's eyes, forcing Wend to carry the conversation. "It's a gift. More comes back to us."

"You're only feeding the ants." He leaned forward, the shadows on his face darkening. "Everything I get, I keep."

The man wolfed down the rabbit, then seized one of two flatbreads from a plate and gnawed off half.

"Anything to drink?" he asked, chewing with his mouth open.

Wend handed him a pitcher of water.

The man sniffed it and set it aside. "Any firewater?"

"Where would we get that?"

The man glanced at Wend's long beard and hair. "No, I guess you wouldn't come by that." He turned to Leena. "Fetch the jug, girl, in my slicker."

Flames shot from Leena's eyes. Her hand inched toward her water cup, made of thick ceramic.

Ketty's voice wailed in Wend's ear: *He won't lift a finger to protect you.*

The man stretched like a bear loosening up for battle. Wend measured him. Wend was taller by six inches, but the man's muscles were bulky, his shoulders so wide and thick that his neck seemed to disappear.

Wend rose quickly. "I'll get it." He found a flask inside the man's coat. Returning to the table, he handed it to him.

The man uncorked the flask. Tipping his head, he took a long pull. "That's a *man's* drink," he said, eyes watering. He held the bottle out to Wend. "Are you a man?"

Wend shook his head.

The man laughed, exposing rotten teeth. "Didn't think so." He took another swig from the flask and looked around the cabin. "This is a right nice place. A man could settle here." His gaze fell on Leena. "Nice 'n sweet."

Leena stood. She swept up the dishes, walked swiftly to the hearth, and began washing them with hot water she kept simmering when it rained.

The man watched her work. Leena was thinner than when they'd first come here, but just as beautiful. Her body was lithe, her curves sensuous. Black hair tumbled in thick coils past her shoulders. Her eyes still shone like gems. Sometimes Wend thought that was just what they were. Eternal orbs bestowed by the gods.

The man plucked two walnuts from a bowl. Squeezing them in his hand, he cracked one of them open.

Lightning flashed. Several seconds later, thunder rumbled, as if the sky were a vast drum.

"Wend," called Leena, "can I speak with you a moment?"

Wend joined her at the hearth. She spoke under her breath. "I want that man out of this house."

"How?" Wend whispered.

"I don't care. Just do it."

"We can't turn him out now, the storm's just getting started."

Leena scrubbed rapidly with a rag. "First thing in the morning, he's gone. Promise me." She looked up at him, fear in her eyes.

Wend laid his cheek against hers. "Promise."

He filled the teapot with hot water, threw in some dried leaves and flowers, and returned to the table with it. He poured two cups. Leena wasn't going to come near the table.

The man ignored the tea. Leaning forward, he said, "Wend . . . that's an unusual name."

"It was my grandfather's."

"I knew a Wend once." His face darkened. *"Wend's Dream.* Is that yours?"

"I think so."

"You don't know?"

"It must be."

"You built it?"

"I don't know."

"You don't know." He looked again at Wend's hair and beard. "I've seen your kind before. Too bad for you." The man took two more walnuts. He squeezed his fist, cracking one of the nuts. "This is a nice cabin, but that b—t's nicer." His gaze traveled back to Leena, running up and down the long curves of her body. "A man could be comfortable on a b—t like that."

Wend's mind raced, searching for a way to tell this man that he had to leave. "We haven't got much here."

The man popped the nut into his mouth, staring coldly at Wend while he chewed.

"That rabbit was the first we've caught."

The man cracked and chewed another nut, his small eyes fixed on Wend.

"We haven't seen fowl, either," said Wend.

The man took another swig from his flask and wiped his mouth on his sleeve.

"And few f—sh," Wend said, stumbling over the word, wishing he could just say it. Feeling that if he could, he would find a missing part of himself. That the numbness and ghosts would go away forever.

The man leaned forward, a nasty gleam in his eyes. "Do you f—sh?"

"No."

"Then how do you know?"

"Leena does."

The man gazed at Leena and licked his lips. "That's a sweet deal."

"We've only got enough for two. That's why our family left."

The man turned back to Wend. "Too bad for you."

"In the morning, you'll have to leave."

To Wend's surprise, the man smiled pleasantly. "Sure, kid. I'll go. First thing in the morning."

Wend lay beneath the furs, Leena cradled in his arms. He had shown the man to the new wing that Dory and Skip had built. A door separated the two rooms, opening toward Wend. There wasn't a latch on either side. There hadn't been any need for one. Before going to bed, Wend had leaned a chair against the door. If the man tried to enter, Wend would hear it. His knife was within reach.

After a spell, Wend had heard the sound of the flask hitting and breaking against a wall. A short time later, the man was snoring.

The fire burned to embers. Leena was quiet, but she wasn't sleeping either. Then, by her breathing, he could tell she was.

The hours ticked by. Rain pelted the cabin. Gusts of wind whistled and shook the shutters.

Wend felt weak, like a small child. He couldn't escape the feeling that the man was laughing at him. Playing with him. Felt he could do whatever he wanted.

Ketty's voice rang in his head: "He won't lift a finger."

But I've never fought anyone, besides that fight with Leena when we were kids. This man has knife scars up and down his hands and arms. How many battles has he fought and survived? Hundreds? What can I do against him?

There's something familiar about him. Why, why can't I remember? It's like it's buried beneath a tangle of thorns.

The wind and rain died down.

Maybe the ghosts will scare him off.

The ghosts were strangely quiet.

The morning was dark and lashed with showers. Wend put a pot of water on the hearth. He took out the last of the pale meat Dory had salted and began cutting it on a board.

"F — sh," he muttered. "Fi — sh."

Leena poured acorn flour from a sack into a bowl. She held the sack upside down, fluttering it to shake out the last of the powder. Her arm dropped in defeat.

"Make as much as you can," said Wend.

"Right." Leena smiled, but Wend saw desperation in her eyes. Unless his traps caught game, they would starve.

"Fi — sh." *Why can't I say it?!*

She added water and began kneading dough. "Should we wake him?" she asked.

"Let him sleep it off," Wend replied. "I don't want to face an angry bear."

"He goes, though. You promised."

"He goes."

Leena punched the dough. "Wend, we need to follow him down to the str — m."

Wend felt himself cringe inside. "Why?"

"He might try to steal the b — t."

Wend didn't know what to say. The water started to simmer and he threw in the salted meat.

"You need to come down with me." Leena slapped a ball of dough until it was flat, and then laid it on a hot skillet.

"What if I freeze?"

"You won't."

"But what if I do?"

"Wait as close as you can. I'll go with him and make sure he leaves. If anything goes wrong, I'll scream."

"What if I can't make my legs move?"

He won't lift a finger to protect you.

"You will."

"But what if I can't."

"You will."

Shortly before noon, the man loomed in the doorway. He growled a perfunctory reply to Wend's good morning, lumbered across the room, and plunked down at the table.

He squinted at the light streaming through the window. "Close that bloody blind."

Wend closed the blind and carried the soup pot to the table.

The man rubbed his temples. His fingertips were pale yellow, his eyes bloodshot. Wend served him soup, high on broth, thin on meat.

"This all you got?" the man grumbled. "What about that rabbit?"

"We finished it last night." Wend handed him a plate of warm flatbread, wrapped in a towel.

The man stuffed bread into his mouth, chasing it down with broth tipped from the bowl. When he was done eating, he wiped his mouth on a grimy shirtsleeve.

Leena had kept her distance, staying busy by the fire. Now she brought a basket to the table. The man followed her with his eyes as she returned to the hearth with his dishes.

"That's some girl you got there," he said.

"She is."

The man turned his attention back to Wend. "I've seen your kind before."

"What kind is that?"

"Hairy men with long beards. They don't have a woman."

Wend didn't know what to say.

The man's gaze ran up and down Leena's body. His hands made little spasmodic motions, as if he were clutching her. "How did someone like you get *that?*"

"I don't know." Wend stood. "There's a break in the rain. We'll walk you down." He handed the man the basket. "The rest of the soup and bread, for your journey."

The man looked inside the basket, surprised. "You're giving it to me?"

"More will come."

The man slapped the basket shut. "It won't. It never does."

The three of them left the cabin. The air was sharp. The smell of rain rose off the red stone. Tall clouds ringing the sky hung motionless.

F – sh, Wend thought. *F – sh.* He peered down at the field. The ghosts were back, babbling. The grass eddied — crazy, random swirls that didn't fit together or match the direction of the wind. For a moment, the field seemed to waver, like the world had when the family disappeared into the heat waves.

Wend stumbled. Leena supported him with both hands.

"Are you all right?" she asked.

"Yes." *F – sh.*

"You look pale."

"I'm all right." *F – sh.*

The man's lip curled up on one side. A disturbing glint came into his eyes.

They reached the trail leading down to the field,

str – m

and a shadow fell across their path; the clouds seemed to have leaped across the sky to hide the sun.

The man pulled up the collar of his slicker. "It's going to rain." His lip curled up farther.

Leena still held Wend's arm. "It'll pass," she said. *F – sh.*

They began climbing down the groove in the cliff. Fine drizzle coated the rock, the man's slicker, and Leena's hair.

"Careful," said Wend. "It's slippery."

The babbling of the ghosts grew louder. The field spun in dizzying spirals. A few fat drops smacked the rock in warning. Then a slant of gray that ran from sky to field rushed toward them. In a moment, they were drenched.

They reached the narrow shelf where (how long ago?) Leena had asked Wend, "Don't you see it?" Her hands had disappeared to the wrist and returned cupping water.

Wend froze, as if his feet were cemented to the rock. A queasy snake twisted in his stomach.

F – sh, f – sh . . .

"What's wrong, kid?" The man's smile broadened. "You're white."

"Nothing." Wend turned to Leena, drinking her in—the brave smile creasing her lips, her gemstone eyes. *Why can't I see the blue in her hair?*

She gripped his arm. She searched his eyes, his face, as if it were the last time she would see him.

He thought she would say something, ask him to go just a little farther. But she reached up, kissed Wend's cheek, and followed the man. A moment later, they disappeared.

Ketty mocked: "He won't lift a finger."

Wend tugged at his feet. *F – sh! F – sh!* His feet had melted into the stone. The rain was a sheet, obscuring the spot where Leena had vanished.

She screamed.

A second later the man yelled in pain. "Bitch!"

Wend's feet were moving before he realized they were free. He didn't know what to expect when he crossed the threshold where the field started. He didn't care about the man. He could come at Wend with a knife. Wend would throw himself on it gladly to save Leena. But if a thousand ghosts rose against him . . .

F – sh, f – sh, F – SH.

The rain lashed. His feet slid on the rock. Then he was past the spot. Light flashed, brighter than the sun, blinding him.

The world came into view. Singing with color. The wind whooshed through the branches of the trees and rustled the leaves. A flock of redwing birds rose from the boughs and chased each other in loops across the sky.

Before him, water surged and danced, sending up sprays of foam and the aroma of mud, earthy and sweet. Rain pocked the water, but the sun peeked from behind a cloud and sparkled on the surface. Something was jumping. Hundreds of them. Rising from the water and diving back in.

F – sh! Fish! STREAM!

He saw a long thread, reaching back to a storm, a boy bobbing in a basket, the love of an old monk, making his first knife, courting Leena, the death of Willow.

He saw it all in a blink, even as his feet plowed through the water. *Wend's Dream* was anchored near the shore. A short dock—Dory must have built it—led to the side of the boat. The man stood behind Leena. He had her arms pinned behind her back with one hand. His other hand was at her neck. Blood streamed down his forearm from two spots on his hand.

Wend leaped onto the dock and ran toward them. "Let her go, Daggitt."

"You know me, boy?" Daggitt laughed. "Then you know I'll snap her neck like a twig."

Wend approached more cautiously. "I know you. You're the coward who bullied children. You're the coward who sneaked in the dark to slit the necks of real men while they slept. You're the coward who stuck a boy on a raft and kicked him downstream without food or water. No fishing pole. No knife. No paddle."

Daggitt grinned, displaying rotten teeth. "Wend?"

"Let her go."

"She goes with me. To do my dirt like you did."

Wend drew closer. "Big, strong Daggitt, cowering behind a woman. Try a man." Wend lifted his hands. "Try these."

Daggitt tossed Leena aside. He lifted his arms above his head. Wend moved in swiftly and they locked hands.

"Looky at you. Wend, a shaggy man."

Daggitt's shoulders swelled, and it felt to Wend as if he were battling a boulder.

The stream exploded around them, sending waves that threatened to sweep over the dock.

"Look at the gifts you got," mocked Daggitt.

Wend slowly bent Daggitt's hands back. Surprise crossed Daggitt's face. Then fear.

"You're wrong." Wend drove him to his knees. "The stream brought *you*."

With a final surge, Wend squeezed. He heard cracking, popping. Daggitt screamed. Wend flung him aside, where he fell in a heap, whimpering over his hands.

Wend ran to Leena and swept her in his arms.

"Forgive me," he cried.

"There's nothing to forgive."

"There is. I failed you and Willow."

"You didn't."

"You must blame me. It's my fault. It's all my fault she died."

"It's not."

Together they sagged to the dock, and Wend sobbed against her breast.

"I didn't protect her, Leena, I didn't protect her."

Chapter Seventeen

The Edge of the World

Wend and Leena bandaged Daggitt's hands. They lingered while the bones knit, feeding him until he could hold a spoon or fork without pain. When they removed the bandages at last, his hands were twisted. He would never crack a nut or snap a neck again. Leaving him fishing gear — "It's more than you gave me," Wend told him — Wend and Leena cast off, letting the stream take them where it would.

Wend had little need for sleep. He rose early so he could gaze upon Leena's face, and they stayed up hours after dark. They talked about little nothings, and nothing felt finer. They lay on their backs gazing at the stars, listening to a night bird sing. They made love, Wend lingering over every inch of Leena's skin and inhaling the scent of her hair.

Tributaries fed into the stream. It broadened, at least a quarter mile across, and on both sides stretched a vast plain.

At winter's end, the stream picked up speed, twisting and turning like a snake. Wend had the sensation that something ahead was drawing him like a monstrous lodestone. The current swelled and plunged. He expected rapids. None came. But the water rushed like the wind, churning and raging violently.

Mist rose in the distance. The stream turned them left and right, but the mist always loomed, rising skyward.

Wend had a bad feeling about that mist. When a natural harbor presented itself, he steered the boat into calm waters and anchored.

Leena gazed with wonder at the mist. "What is it?"

"I'm guessing a waterfall," Wend replied.

"What do we do? We can't go back."

Wend studied the shoreline, where cordage grass rustled, and beyond, alders and sycamores grew thick as weeds.

"We could hike forward and investigate," said Wend.

"Then we couldn't return to the boat."

"Remember when I was tramping around the forest behind the cabin? I found I could go three miles."

"What if we go too far?"

"We won't. My legs know three miles."

"I knew there was a reason I married you." Leena laughed.

They packed lunch and set out on a narrow track through the trees. The first few miles were peaceful. Birds flitted among the branches. Squirrels raced up and down tree trunks, chattering at them. But a distant, rolling thunder grew to a roar. By the time they left the trees, they needed to shout to hear each other.

They crossed a flat stretch of granite, slick with mist, and stopped. The world plunged before them, as if the gods had sliced it away. To their right, the plain extended to the horizon. To their left, the stream rushed over the edge, sending up spray a thousand feet.

Leena gripped Wend's arm with both hands. "I've never seen anything like it," she said.

"I don't think there *is* anything like it." He peered down through the mist. "I can't see the bottom. Oh, Leena, how many boats have fallen to ruin here? What if the myths are true, and the stream does end at the edge of the world?"

She took his hand in her own and drew it toward her until it lay on her belly. "I know this. *Wend's Dream* doesn't end here."

Wend gazed at her belly. "You mean . . ."

She smiled up at him. "Where there's life, there's hope."

❖

On the journey back to the boat, they weighed their options. The cliff was too steep to climb down. They could only hike three miles across the plateau. If they couldn't find a passage down, they couldn't return to the boat. They could disassemble the boat and try to lower it on ropes, as Skip had many years before, but neither Wend or Leena believed they could weave a rope long enough. And they had to get down themselves.

If there was a bottom . . .

Leena knit her brow, and as the sun set, the furrows deepened. "Do you think my parents and Dory came this way? It's too awful to think they might have gone over."

"We passed a fork upstream. Maybe they went that way." But Wend couldn't help thinking that all paths led here.

That night, as Leena lay breathing softly in his arms, Wend's mind drifted back to Dory — how he would roll a flame around the bowl of his pipe, and then send up a cloud of smoke. Wend slipped into a deep sleep, and toward morning he dreamed about the cabin, and how he had found a tall basket filled with water beside the one he'd woven.

He sat up with a start. "That's it!"

❖

Wend pulled two juicy trout off the grill and slid them onto plates. The harbor was loaded with fish, and he'd caught these within minutes.

"You've kept me in suspense long enough," said Leena, as she dived into her breakfast. "Tell me your idea or I'll look for another husband."

Wend laughed. "It's simple. We go over in a basket."

She stopped eating and stared at him. "You're crazy."

"Am I? Yours never leak. And they float."

"We could die. There must be another way."

"I'm all ears." Wend speared a chunk of fish, and inhaled the aroma before popping it into his mouth. He chewed slowly, relishing the smoky flavor. "We can stay here until the end of the dry season. That gives you time to make a basket big enough for both of us. Meanwhile, we have plenty of fish and can trap game in the trees."

Leena tapped her fork. "We can't stay here forever. The stream will shake us loose."

"The stream will shake us loose."

She rose. Stepping closer, she leaned over and cradled his head against her bosom. "I can't think of anyone I'd rather share a basket with."

The days were full, so full they seemed empty of time. If not for the heat and the falling water level, Wend wouldn't have marked the end of summer. The stream was almost tame, flowing at a crisp pace, without the turbulence and chaos of winter.

Wend fished, set traps, and cut bundles of cordage grass. At night, they twisted the cordage Leena needed. By day, her fingers flew at the basket.

The moment the basket was finished, which was early, Wend and Leena were glued to each other. They swam in the clear waters of the harbor, schools of iridescent fish swirling around them. They took long walks in the forest and made love in a meadow of flowers. They danced beneath the stars.

The water level dropped. Islands rose from the stream. The wind shifted. Wend smelled rain and knew it was time to go.

They hiked to the edge of the waterfall one last time, to see how much power the dry season had sapped from the stream. They sat when they reached the edge of the rock, both of them silent and lost in thought. Stars glimmered above. The cataract was a mysterious, cyanine blue in the moonlight.

"What do we do with the boat?" Leena asked at last.

"Leave it," Wend replied. "Maybe it will help some other traveler."

Leena nodded toward the water and placed her palm protectively on her belly. "It's not much tamer."

Wend studied the stream. The waterfall sent up massive spray, not as high as the first time they'd come here, but towering, nonetheless. The current raced, as if the force of every stream above was concentrated here. A mast and crossbeam tumbled in the turbulence. A wave swept over it. Wend tried holding his breath while it was submerged. He exhaled before the mast surfaced. It broke water at last like a gigantic bird, the crossbeam flopping like a broken wing.

Leena gasped. "If a mast can shatter, how will a basket survive?"

"Dory once told me that the strongest boat he ever saw was made from reeds."

"Why?"

"Trees are land plants, stiff and unyielding. Cordage grass is a daughter of the stream, bending with the current."

Leena clutched his arm. "Maybe we should stay."

"You know we can't. You said it yourself. The stream will shake us loose."

"Maybe it won't."

"The rocks around the harbor aren't very high. The first flood will overrun them and sweep us away. Now's our chance."

She shivered. "What will happen to us?"

Wend put his arms around her and drew her close. "I don't know. All we can do is throw ourselves on the stream and see where it leads."

❖

Rocks, thrusting into the stream like a thumb and forefinger trying to meet, formed the harbor. They brought the basket to the stream side of the rocks and set it down on a flat spot. They had practiced the launch dozens of times on the harbor side. Wend was certain it would run smoothly.

The stream looked peaceful. Wend knew this was deceptive. The light of dawn muted shapes and shadows.

He gazed at *Wend's Dream* for the last time, and turned to the task at hand.

The basket was oval, wide and tall enough for them to sit in. He didn't want extra room for them to rattle in, and Leena had padded the inside with cushions to protect their backs and heads. Deep inside one of the cushions was a sheathed knife.

He climbed onto rocks that were slightly above the opening of the basket and jumped inside. Leena sat on the rocks, feet dangling. Wend reached up and helped her down. The lid, fastened to one side, was pulled shut. Leena wove it into place.

Wend folded his arms and legs around Leena. She hugged him about the middle. Together, rocking back and forth, they tipped the basket into the stream. The current snatched them up, but the basket righted, top to sky.

The Stream

The stream bubbled and boiled, bouncing, tossing, spinning them. Wend drew Leena closer, his arms enveloping her protectively.

Despite the turbulence, he felt strangely at peace. He had surrendered. The rest was up to the stream.

The morning sun passed through the translucent walls of the basket. He drank in Leena's face. He caressed her hair, softer than down. The girl who had trembled beside him last night was gone. The old, brave Leena smiled up at him.

His heart swelled. Nothing else existed.

This moment—

the stream,

the sun,

the basket,

Leena,

her breath against his cheek—

The stream crashed and boomed around them. He could hear himself breathe as they were submerged beneath the waves, only to be flung up again into rolling chaos. Roaring grew in the distance. When it was almost deafening, Wend figured they were near the crest of the waterfall.

Thunder exploded around them. They shot into the air.

"I love you," he yelled, aware that she couldn't hear him. Then they were falling . . .

Falling . . .

Falling . . .

He found her lips, and thought, *Sweet.* . . .

Epilogue

Flames flickered about the remains of the logs. I paused, my voice grown hoarse with the telling. One of the men handed me a mug of tea, and I sipped from it, gratefully.

"How does it end?" she asked, her first words of the night. Her hands were nestled in her lap, her thumb long uprooted from her mouth. The stuffed rabbit lay forgotten at her feet.

"There's not much more to tell."

"Did they live?" she asked. "Did she have the baby?"

"He cut them out of the basket. They lingered at the base of the waterfall, where she bore him a son, and a year later, another. He built another boat and went with the current, for it wasn't the edge of the world, and the stream flowed on."

"Did they ever see Dory and her parents again?"

"Some say they did."

"What do you say?"

It was a few short hours to dawn. The others drifted away

to spread out bedrolls for the night. The narrow-eyed man had gone to sleep long ago.

"That maybe it's time for bed," I replied. "You can sleep here, by the fire." What more could I say? Some of it I saw, some I was told, and some I imagined.

She nodded, curled up at my feet, and I covered her with my blanket. I handed her the box. Faint scratching came from within. She removed the lid. A feathery bundle struggled up, its beak spread wide for food.

"We'll look for worms tomorrow," I said. "You keep the baby safe." And I'll watch over both of you, I thought.

She replaced the lid, cradled the box in her arms, and soon she slumbered.

I stoked the fire to keep her warm, reflecting on how the stream had softened me. As night melted into dawn, I too, fell asleep.

She roused me with a desperate shake at my foot, and pointed. All but the narrow-eyed stranger had departed, and he was gliding away on my skiff.

He pulled his knife from his boot top and waved it, as if beckoning me to try to stop him. "Nothing's free, old man. This is payment for that duck."

"It seems we've found our thief," I called back.

I stood, and she tugged at my pant leg. "Can't we stop him?" she cried.

"Let him go."

"But your boat . . ." Tears pooled in her eyes as she watched him drift away. "It's my fault you lost it."

The Stream

"We'll do just fine." I opened my rucksack and pulled out my drop line. "See?"

We found worms under a log, and while I fished off the rocks, she sat beside me feeding her bird.

After breakfast, she touched one of the holes in my mittens. "I could knit you another pair."

"Do you remember what Dory said when Wend tried to clean up after their first breakfast?"

She looked up at me, her round eyes as blue as the sky. "That Wend wasn't his servant." She smiled. "How long will I be staying?"

She had been hurt enough. No part of me wished to harm or frighten her further. As easy as it would have been to say, "As long as you like," I had to do one more thing, and sooner rather than later, or else she might have doubts about me.

"You know what's inside these mittens?"

She nodded.

"And that doesn't scare you?"

She shook her head. "Let me see them."

"They are frightfully ugly."

"It's okay," she said, softly. With the same care she used with the fallen bird, she pulled off both mittens, revealing the twisted hands Wend had left me.

No one knows better than I the dark places a man may hide. The things a man may do. Nothing washes them away, and they burn forever. But with the first clumsy attempts at fishing, sight returned to a man blinded by a black vision of the world.

Life sends what we need. I don't understand the how or the why, only that small, fragile gifts offset the terrible things that befall us.

I squandered one precious gift, before, kicking him downstream on a raft. I wouldn't lose this one. Hoisting her on my shoulders, I stepped into the stream.

BOOK CLUB QUESTIONS

1. How is the stream a character in the story? What is it a metaphor for?

2. Explore the ways various characters have a limited vision of reality. How does this impact their life on the stream, limit their experiences in the world, and cause them suffering?

3. At one point, Leena suggests that the stream makes strays out of all of us. What does she mean, and what is its significance?

4. Wend says Leena is the diamond from the monks' Stone Dance. Who else in the novel does the stream reveal as a diamond. How does the stream eventually reveal the diamond in each of us?

5. What do you think of the choice Leena makes to stay with Wend? What is the author saying about love and loyalty in relationships?

6. What does Wend have at the end of the tale that he didn't have before?

7. How does the story within a story amplify the thematic and emotional power of the novel?

If you enjoyed *The Stream,* please suggest it to your book club! To arrange an author visit, live or virtual, email him at contact@arsilverberry.com. Enjoy the first two chapters of A. R. Silverberry's award-winning novel, *Wyndano's Cloak,* in the pages ahead!

Preview Selection From

A. R. Silverberry's

Wyndano's Cloak

Available Now

1

The warning whispered in the leaves rustling in a windless dawn. Jen always knew it would come, but the danger had drifted to the back of her mind like a fading nightmare, leaving only a vague clutching beneath the common activities of the day.

She'd been running along the western side of King's Loop, dawn just pushing above the Aedilac Mountains. Silhouettes streaked by, a farmhouse, a barn, a peach orchard heavy with fruit. Her hair streamed behind, catching the wind like a sail. She almost flew, feet barely touching the ground.

Kicking up a cloud of dirt, she veered off the road and cut through a meadow. She spread her arms, feeling the waist-high grass brush her palms as she whizzed by. Leaving the meadow, she ducked into a thicket of trees, dodging low-lying limbs with the thrill of a bird that's found its wings.

She broke into a clearing and headed toward a stream. With a surge she leaped over the water and made for the lone oak near the bank. Here, a ring of rocks collected water in a quiet pool. Only a few hungry skeeter hawks skated across the surface, looking for an early breakfast. Ducks slept in the grass. They raised their heads and started waddling toward her as she untied a leather pouch.

Taking out a handful of breadcrumbs, she flung it to them. They scrambled with straining necks and blaring trumpets. She threw some toward a runt standing uncertainly on the side, but a big white quacker beat him off with a showy rattle of wings.

Jen pretended to slip the food back in her pocket and waited until the others glided into the water. Then she poured the crumbs into her hand and held it out. The runt hesitated, then crept forward until his beak nibbled her palm.

"You're small," she said softly, "but you can be quick. Dart between them."

When the food was gone, she leaned against the tree. King's Loop looked like a ribbon from here, winding through farm and woodland until it met the great gates of Glowan. There it zigzagged through the little town until it came to the Rose Castle, shining like a jewel in the rising sun. The sheer cliff beyond beckoned. She looked away and exhaled, sighing with frustration and longing.

That was when she heard the whispering. Alert, she backed away from the tree and studied it at a crouch. The air was still. The grass motionless. But the leaves stirred and fluttered. Words floated down. At first they were indistinct, as if someone called through a distant snowstorm. One word emerged clearly, and an icy finger traced down her spine.

She heard her name.

She backed away until she squatted on some rocks that extended into the pool. Every muscle—sun-hammered and wind-hardened like metal in a forge—was poised to spring. Phrases whispered down. The only sense she could make was that something was coming. Something dangerous.

She thought of her family. Fear tightened around her heart. She was a hair's-breadth away from running to them. Her feet stayed rooted to the spot. Maybe she'd hear more.

A small splash made her look at the pond. Two more followed, as if someone had thrown pebbles. Nothing had fallen into the water. But ripples spread out and ran into each other. More splashes erupted like tiny volcanoes, until the whole pool was agitated with colliding rings. A circle of calm emerged below Jen's feet, pushing the waves back. Pale and ghostly, a face rose from the muddy bottom of the pool until it floated just below the surface. Little hills and valleys lined the features of an old woman, as if olives lay under the skin.

"Medlara." Jen spoke under her breath, unwilling to believe her friend could hear her.

Medlara smiled, but her expression hardened. Words whispered from the pool. Jen leaned forward, straining to hear. She got little more than fragments, as if a storyteller jumbled the pieces of a tale. One phrase repeated, like a riddle. "If you meet . . . a harp, you must . . . If the worst happens, seek the answers—"

Jen dropped to her knees, hoping to catch more. Medlara's hands appeared just below her chin. She clasped them, and lifted her eyes as if she were imploring Jen. She mouthed two words. They might have been, "Forgive me."

Streaks of blue snaked and flowered in the water, as if someone had dropped in dye. Tendrils of mist rose from the surface and licked the ring of rocks. Soon the whole pool was covered. Spilling over the edge, the cloudy vapor surrounded Jen. She backed onto the shore, but the stuff sprouted up on all sides, walling her in, and formed a ceiling above. It crept along the ground until it met her feet. There it paused like an undulating sea.

Jen studied the mist. "She's trying to show me something. But what?"

There was no time to wonder. Fog rose before her like a giant shadow. Black. Forbidding . . .

She stepped back. Looked behind for an escape route. The fog surged forward and pulled her into the inky darkness. She could no longer feel the ground, as if everything solid and beautiful that she cared about was being ripped away. She tried to scream but terror rose from the pit of her stomach and froze in her throat.

The rest was a dizzy kaleidoscope of tilting and falling, of wandering lost, with no way out, no way home, no way back to a world of light and love, until the mist melted away and she collapsed, shaking in a pool of sweat.

* * *

How long she lay there she couldn't say, but at last she stopped trembling, her heart slowed, and she gulped some big breaths of air and rose. She staggered to the pool. It looked ordinary enough now. A handful of skeeter hawks glided peacefully on the surface.

The morning sun of Aerdem sparkled on the stream. A few birds sang in the tree. Shaking off numb shock, she splashed water on her face, wiped her hands on her breeches, and ran for King's Loop. She streaked through the fields and leaped onto the road, where a few farmers were carting goods to market. Tearing past them, she was vaguely aware they'd stopped to bow to the king's daughter.

2

Jen wanted to run the full length of the castle directly to her father. But she didn't want to attract attention. Instead, she walked briskly through the corridors. The castle was buzzing with activity. Servants whisked carts of linen or trays of bread and fruit down the halls. A crew of carpenters carried lumber for construction on a new library. Jen could hear the rap of hammers in a room beyond. Everyone smiled and bowed when she passed. She smiled back, trying to hide the cold shivers running through her.

She thought she knew what the danger was. The whole family would guess the same thing. There was only one thing that could threaten them.

But how would it happen? And when?

She eyed the castle wall. Deep inside the translucent stone, green and turquoise flickered and shimmered like fire. Jen heaved a sigh of relief. Red-hot flames would have meant the danger was upon them.

Still, Medlara hadn't taken the time to send a messenger. That could only mean one thing. Whatever was going to happen would occur in a few days.

Jen had to understand what Medlara had shown her. As frightening as it was, she forced herself to relive it in her mind. One memory stood out. She'd been seized. Held powerless. Then thrown like a sack of potatoes. Was that a way of saying the family might lose control of the throne? Could be overthrown? That didn't seem likely. Since the family had been reunited, after years of separation, Aerdem had prospered. Her father was a popular king.

She stepped into an inner courtyard used as an open-air market for the small city of nobles, servants, and emissaries that lived in the castle. Cobblers, fishmongers, tailors, candlemakers, potters, and a dozen others bargained with customers at stalls around the edges of the square.

Jen approached a man hawking flowers, and purchased a spray of marigolds for her father. When she reached the end of the courtyard she hesitated, fingering the vertical scar across her left eyebrow while she tottered between two routes. The fastest way to her father was to the right, across the walkways and bridges. In the past, Jen would dash across these, leaping from merlon to merlon, or tightrope-walking the handrails like a daredevil. She longed to do that again, but a wave of dizziness turned her left into a safe inner corridor.

Father would want to call a family meeting. This route would take Jen past Bit's apartment. Aside from being Jen's best friend, Bit was engaged to Dash, Jen's half brother. Everyone would want to include Bit.

Jen turned left again onto the corridor leading to Bit's apartment. Ahead, standing in front of Bit's door, a girl argued with a servant. Her back was to Jen, but the strawberry blonde ringlets falling to the shoulders made her instantly recognizable as Countess Petunia Pompahro.

"Let me in this instant, you impertinent thing," the Countess scolded.

"I can't, Miss. Bit has forbidden anyone to enter," replied the servant, a girl about twelve with an oval face and button nose. Her blue eyes challenged the Countess defiantly.

"It's Lady Bit to you," said the Countess. "If you were my servant, I'd have you flogged for talking like that. Now open that door or I will have you flogged."

"She doesn't mind me calling her Bit. She insists I call her that," the girl replied boldly.

"I don't care. Now open the door."

"No, Miss. No one's to pass."

"I'll be the judge of that. I'm quite sure she did not mean me. Step aside. I am one of Bit's closest confidantes."

"Perhaps, but you're not going through this door. Bit is working on a surprise and no one's to see it 'til it's done."

By this time Jen had joined them. "It's okay, Sally. Let Bit know I'm here."

Sally nodded and stepped inside the room.

Petunia turned to Jen and gave a slight curtsy. "You really must take a firmer hand with your domestics."

Jen ignored the remark. Petunia's long nose and chin—which would be cute on a poodle—did nothing to flatter the Countess. Her only attractive feature was her long lashes, which she fluttered like an agitated butterfly whenever a handsome gentleman passed. She never lost a chance to flutter them at Dash, even though he was engaged to Bit.

Bit peeked shyly out the door. "Jenny! Pet! Are you here to see me?" Bit's soft, brown eyes were wide and earnest.

"Of course we are." Petunia smoothed her dress. "Why wouldn't we come to see you? We're friends, aren't we?"

Bit's face lit up. "Wonderful. Give me a second, I'll be right out."

A moment later, Bit stepped out, leaving the door ajar. Petunia craned her head to see what was in the room.

"Bit," Jen said, "can you come with me to the Crystal Room? I'm calling a family meeting."

"Sure. What's it about?"

"I'll tell you when we get there."

"Is something wrong?" Petunia pried.

Jen eyed the Countess and shrugged. "No. Just family stuff."

"I'm so glad to see you both," Bit said. "I'm planning a surprise birthday party for Dash and want to know what you think of my idea."

"Maybe that should wait," said Jen, taking Bit's arm and trying to lead her down the hall.

But Pet grabbed the other arm and stopped them. "No. Let's hear all about it."

Bit smiled, her face warm and dreamy. "I thought I'd throw a cozy affair in the Hearth Room. Just family and a few close friends. Jenny, I thought your mom and I could cook Dash's favorite recipes. You know how he's always asking me to learn them. Then we can sing some songs by the fire, and after dessert, I'm going to give him this."

Bit looked around to make sure no one was looking, then pulled a velvet pouch from her pocket.

"What is it?" asked Petunia.

"I made it myself," whispered Bit. "It's not quite done." She untied the leather strings at the top of the pouch and pulled out an exact replica of the castle: the walkways, courtyards, towers and spires, the gardens and fountains, it was all there.

"Bit!" Jen exclaimed. "That's incredible! How did you do that?"

Bit blushed. "Do you really like it? I still need to carve the windows and glue on the flags. I thought if I put it over a small candle, it would glow, just like the Rose Castle."

Petunia stroked her chin shrewdly. "You could make a bundle selling them. I wouldn't ask less than thirty gold petals apiece."

"Oh, I don't think I could make another. This one took me far too long." Bit looked proudly at the carving, then returned it to the pouch.

"You know, Bit," said Petunia, "you really ought to wear a white sash instead of that blue belt."

Bit looked down at her belt. She wore a long, airy, white gown, and the belt gathered snugly around her elfin waist.

"What's wrong with it?" she asked, as if she had done something terrible. "I thought these were popular."

"No one's going to be wearing those anymore. Vieveeka—a duchess from Trilafor—is visiting Father and me. She's really quite wonderful and knows all kinds of important people. She says that in the courts of Laskamont and Trilafor everyone is wearing sashes, and that belts, especially blue belts, are totally passé. See? Look at mine."

"I . . . didn't know," said Bit, her eyes growing large. "Should I change it? I wouldn't want Dash to see me in anything . . . old-fashioned."

Jen looked at Petunia's sash. It did look striking against the Countess' scarlet dress. But Bit needed no style consultant. Her thick auburn hair fell in heavy tresses over her shoulders, framing a creamy complexion broken only by a whisper of freckles. Nothing looked bad on Bit, who moved with the mysterious grace of a forest fairy. She was the most beautiful girl Jen had ever seen, except perhaps Jen's mother.

"You look fine, Bit," Jen said. She had to find a way to ditch Petunia, who was becoming a nuisance. Jen grabbed Bit's arm again and turned down the corridor. Pet followed at their heels.

"Pet, could you do me a big favor?" Jen asked. "It would save me a trip if you'd let the Pondit know the family is meeting in the Crystal Room."

Pet wrinkled her nose. "That old fool. What does anyone want with him?"

"He's Chief Counselor to my father. You know that."

"He's old and his clothes smell. I wish I could help you, but I just remembered, I have to run an errand for my father. I'd go to your Pondit, but it's really in the wrong direction. Well, see you later."

With a rustle of her gown, the Countess took off in the other direction down the hall, pausing only to flutter her long lashes at a handsome duke.

Jen hurried forward, tugging Bit with her. When she was sure that Petunia was out of sight, she pulled Bit aside.

"I wouldn't confide so much in Petunia if I were you," Jen said.

"Why? What have I done?"

"Maybe nothing. But I don't think she's really your friend."

"I thought she was. She's always nice to me."

"Always?" Jen asked. "Was she nice before you became engaged to Dash?"

"That's different. I suppose it was right for a countess to treat me like a servant. I was a servant."

"You don't treat any of the servants that way, do you?"

Bit shook her head.

"Neither do I," Jen said. "Or Dash, or my father or mother." She hurried forward again, pulling Bit along.

"What's wrong, Jenny? Has something happened? You're acting strange."

Jen chose her words carefully. "Something might happen. Something bad. I'll tell you more when we're all together."

"Is it about Dash?" Bit asked. She twisted a corner of her dress as she trotted to keep up. "Is Dash all right?"

"It's about all of us. None of us may be safe."

Bit stopped and clutched the top of her collar. She leaned against a wall, her face white. "Jenny. You're scaring me."

"I'm sorry, Bit. I didn't mean to. Maybe it'll turn out to be nothing." Jen didn't think so, but Bit was no good to her like this. "Mom and Dad will know what to do."

Bit nodded absently, her face still pale.

"Bit, I need you to do something for me. Go to the south wing and tell the Pondit to meet us in the Crystal Room. And send a message to my mom and Dash."

Bit agreed, and Jen watched her walk, still dazed, down the corridor. Jen turned a corner and hurried in the other direction. She worried about Bit. Bit was fragile and delicate. But she would need to be strong. They all would, if they were to get through what lay ahead.

Jen made her way up several stories to the east wing. She slowed when she reached the stairs leading to the Crystal Room. It wasn't the lack of a banister on the right that bothered her. She could take stairs without getting dizzy. It was her father. How would he react to the news? He had been strong, once. But he had been broken. Broken by the very thing Jen now feared. He was healing, but how would this affect him?

Now that she was here, Jen went up the stairs reluctantly. The door at the top was closed. She hesitated, biting her lower lip. With a deep breath she turned the handle and slipped silently into the room. Her father was playing a lute, his eyes closed as he listened to the vibration of the strings. Jen moved quietly past and sat on a loveseat opposite him.

The Crystal Room had become her father's workshop. By the window a telescope angled toward the sky. A desk in one corner had two large volumes, one of poetry, the other her father's journal. Behind were the makings of a small library. On the other side of the room was a wooden table. A sextant, a globe, and a large map were spread on top. A series of shelves, rising from floor to ceiling, were lined with antique objects. Her father said most of them had a purpose long forgotten. Several were laid out on the table and disassembled. On a small end table were a cup and teapot decorated with roses. The scent of lemon slices filled the air.

She listened as he played, feeling the tension in her shoulders relax. His hands caressed and stroked the strings, making them sing and sigh. He struck the last chord with a flourish. When the notes faded, he looked up and smiled at her.

"That was beautiful," she said. "I liked the part where your thumb kept brushing the bass note."

"Most people miss that," he replied. "It takes a subtle thumb, listening to the other fingers, supporting them in what they do so the whole piece is unified."

"Sort of like the way you rule."

He looked at her curiously. "I could never rule Aerdem alone. I need all five fingers. Perhaps I was the thumb once. But now Dash is, sturdy and reliable."

"Then who's the forefinger?" Jen asked with a laugh.

"You are. Strong. Agile. Never backing off. I'm the fourth finger. Musicians call that the poet."

"That fits."

"Your mother is the middle finger. Being in the center, she is the heart in all we do."

"So Bit's the pinky."

"Right. It's the weakest finger, but the hand is stronger because it has one."

"What would a hand be without a pinky?" She laughed.

They rose and she handed him the bouquet of marigolds. After placing them in a vase, he hugged her tight. Tilting her head up, he smiled as he looked into her eyes.

"Green, with flecks of fire, just like your mother," he said.

She gazed back and studied his face. He was ruggedly handsome, his features chiseled with a few perfect strokes. Jet-black hair, just beginning to frost around the edges, fell in loose curls over his forehead. He was sensitive and gentle, yet underneath she felt his strength and power. Still, she hesitated to tell him what had brought her there.

"You're up early," he said.

"Uh-huh. The carpenters are making progress on the new library. I saw them moving a lot of lumber for shelves." She shifted her feet, unable to calm the feelings boiling inside.

"Jenny, is there something wrong? You can tell me."

Still she hesitated, looking into his magnetic gray eyes, searching for some sign of how he would take it. "I got a message . . ." Once started she couldn't stop. It came pouring out. The whispering leaves. The wall of fog. The inky darkness. Medlara's face rising from the muddy bottom of the pool.

And there was her father—strong, commanding, and kingly—falling to the sofa, clutching his hand to his throat.

Wyndano's Cloak

Gift Edition

Limited edition hardbacks are only available through the author, at www.arsilverberry.com. Get your signed or unsigned collectible copy now!

Ebook Editions

Ebook editions are available through Amazon, Barnes and Noble, and iTunes.

ACKNOWLEDGMENTS

Thanks always go first to my wife, Sherry, who often understands my work better than I do. Her insight and feedback kept me on track and raised the bar. I'm fortunate to have two expert sets of eyes in my editors, Walter Kleine and Mark Rhynsberger, who scoured the manuscript for all those little things, and helped me tighten it. I'm especially indebted to Mark, who helped me clarify the writing, and hung in there when I was slow on the uptake. Any remaining errors are mine. My beta readers, Linda Ginsberg, Elisa Adler (a fabulous writer), Selena Jayo, and Elle Thornton (another fabulous writer), provided invaluable feedback. I'm grateful to Diane Whiddon (Novel Website Design) for nailing the ebook cover, to Fostering-Success for the softback interior design, and to Ray Fowler (Fowler Digital Services) for the ebook design.

I'm indebted to the following sources for helping me understand Wend's world. Jay Daniel helped me understand sailboats, and the river trip I took with him and his father some forty-five years ago seeded the story. Primitiveways.com and Hedgehogleatherworks.com helped me understand such things as spear, rope, knife, and basket making. The following sources helped me understand how to make a dugout canoe: Primitiveways.com; *How to Make a Dugout Canoe,* by Jim McDowell January/February 1984, Mother Earth; *Making a Dugout Canoe*, blog post by Will Hormley; and *The Dugout Canoe Project*, by Mike Volmar, which had outstanding archeological and historical references. Two websites, Babyswimming.com and Infantswim.com, helped me understand what infants, toddlers, and small children are capable of doing in the water, and of the ways to protect children from drowning accidents.

Nothing in this book was intended as a criticism of any religion or religious group; in particular, of Buddhism, whose philosophy and stories inspired the novel. My thanks to their monks for letting me borrow their colorful robes.

ABOUT THE AUTHOR

A. R. Silverberry's novel, WYNDANO'S CLOAK, won the Gold Medal in the 2011 Benjamin Franklin Awards for Juvenile/Young Adult Fiction; the Gold Medal in the 2010 Readers Favorite Awards for Preteen Fiction; and the Silver Medal in the 2011 Bill Fisher Award for Best First Book, Children's/Young Adult. He lives in California, where the majestic coastline, trees, and mountains inspire his writing. *THE STREAM* is his second novel. Follow him at www.arsilverberry.com.

ABOUT TREE TUNNEL PRESS

Tree Tunnel Press publishes fiction and nonfiction books. We are interested in the power of art and culture to positively impact society. We create products that entertain, encourage, and inspire. Requests for rights or permissions should be directed to: Tree Tunnel Press P.O. Box 733 Capitola, CA 95010

Visit our website, www.treetunnelpress.com, for more information.

Made in the USA
Charleston, SC
04 June 2014